9016132635

Book 1

Miss Annie
FREEDOM!

Frank Le Gall
Illustrated by **Flore Balthazar**
Coloring by **Robin Doo**

Graphic Universe™ • Minneapolis • New York

Story by Frank Le Gall
Art by Flore Balthazar
Coloring by Robin Doo

Translation by Carol Klio Burrell

English translation copyright © 2012 by Lerner Publishing Group, Inc.

First American edition published in 2012 by Graphic Universe™. Published by arrangement with MEDIATOON LICENSING – France.

Miss Annie
© DUPUIS 2010 – Balthazar & Le Gall
www.dupuis.com

Graphic Universe™ is a trademark of Lerner Publishing Group, Inc.

Graphic Universe™
A division of Lerner Publishing Group, Inc.
241 First Avenue North
Minneapolis, MN 55401 U.S.A.

Website address: www.lernerbooks.com

Library of Congress Cataloging-in-Publication Data

Le Gall, Frank, 1959–
      Freedom! / by Frank Le Gall ; illustrated by Flore Balthazar.
        p.   cm. – (Miss Annie ; #1)
      Summary: At four months of age, Miss Annie the kitten is eager to leave her masters' house and find freedom in the outdoors, but she soon learns that there are important rules to be followed there, as well.
        ISBN: 978-0-7613-7884-6 (lib. bdg. : alk. paper) 1. Graphic novels. [1. Graphic novels.
      2. Cats–Fiction. 3. Animals–Infancy–Fiction. 4. Mice–Fiction.] I. Balthazar, Flore, ill. II. Title.
      PZ7.7.L42Fre 2012
      741.5′973–dc23   2011021726

Manufactured in the United States of America
1 – DP – 12/31/11

1. Home Alone

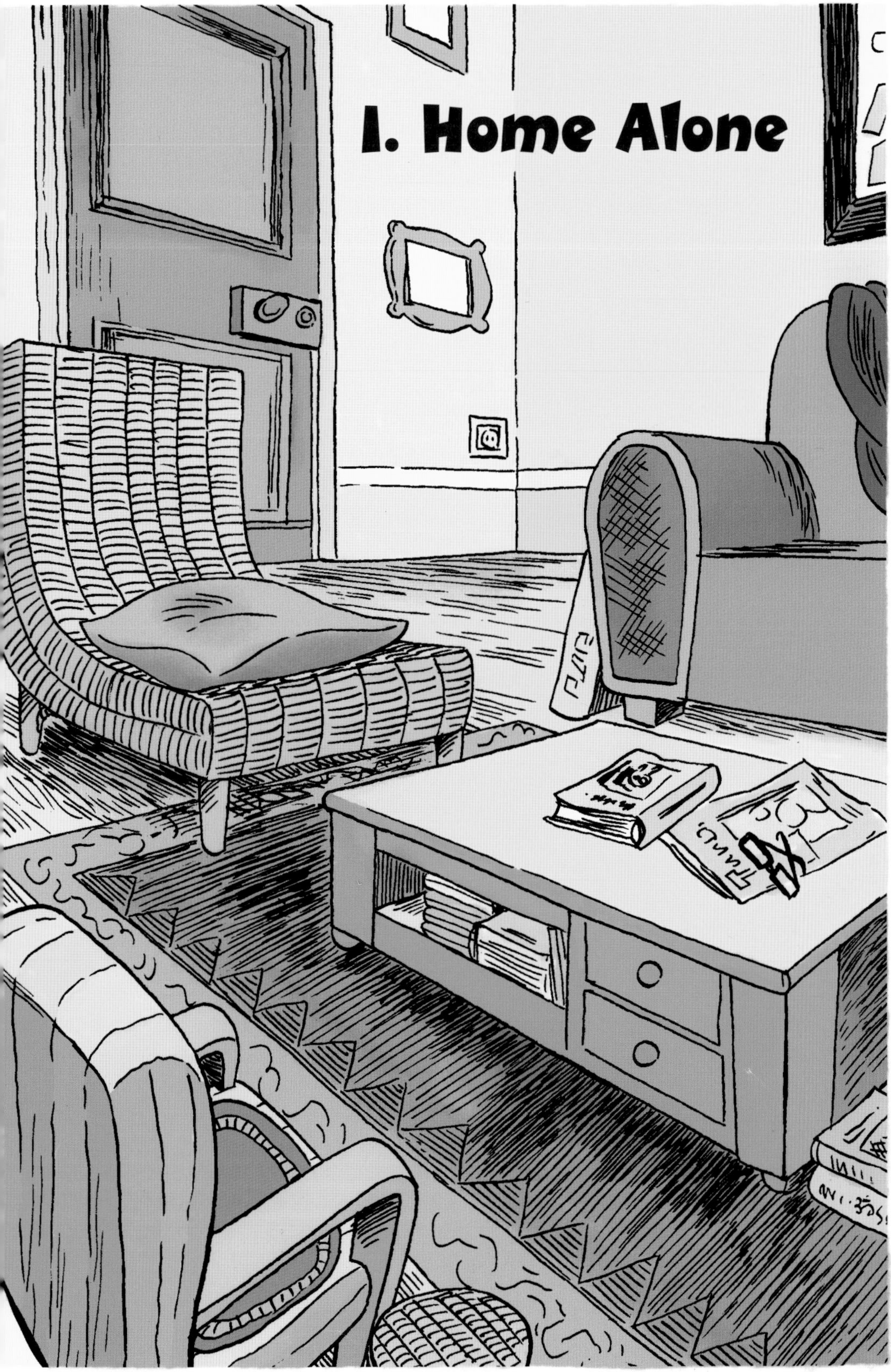

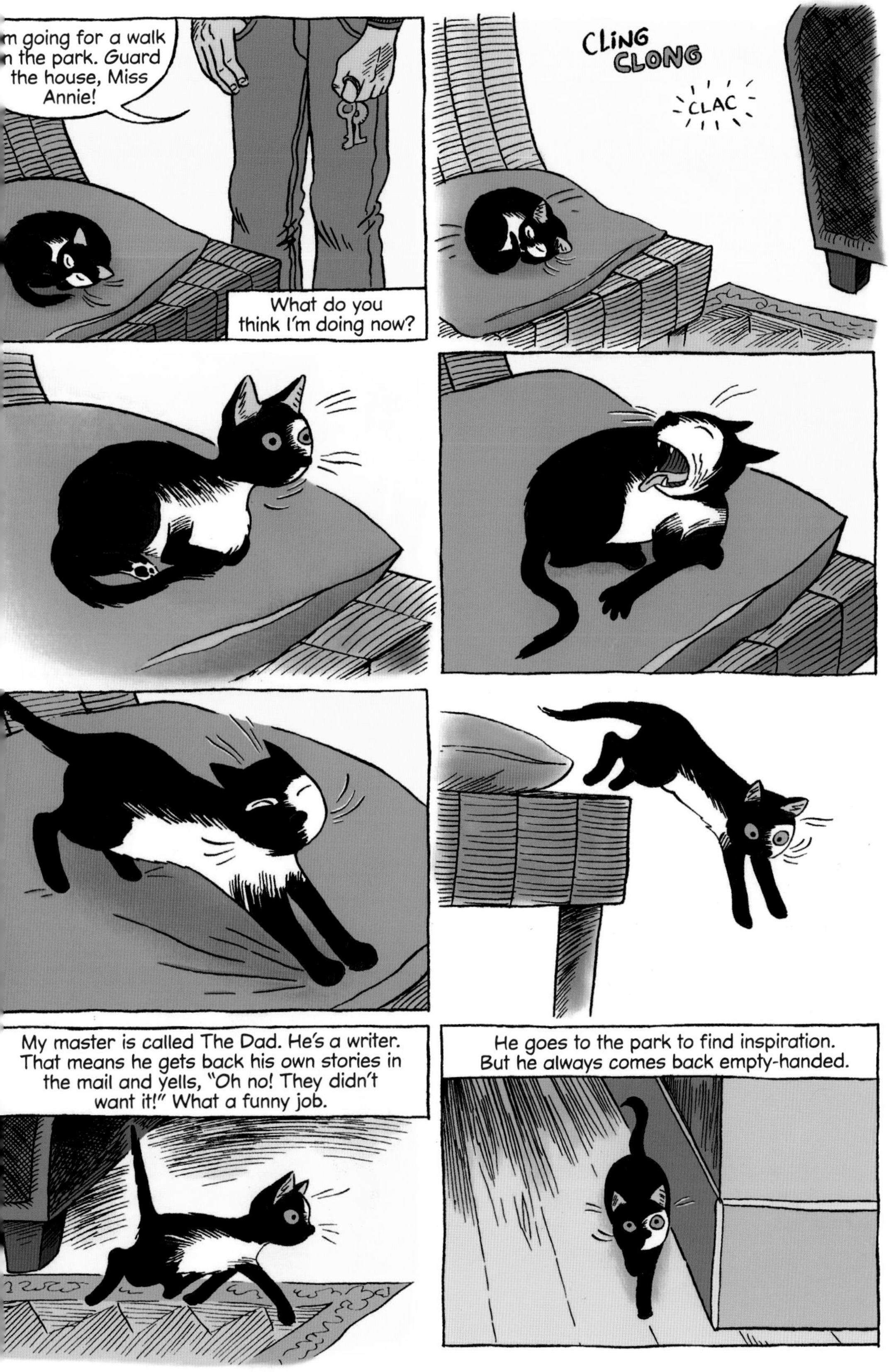
m going for a walk
n the park. Guard
the house, Miss
Annie!
What do you
think I'm doing now?
CLING
CLONG
CLAC
My master is called The Dad. He's a writer. That means he gets back his own stories in the mail and yells, "Oh no! They didn't want it!" What a funny job.
He goes to the park to find inspiration. But he always comes back empty-handed.

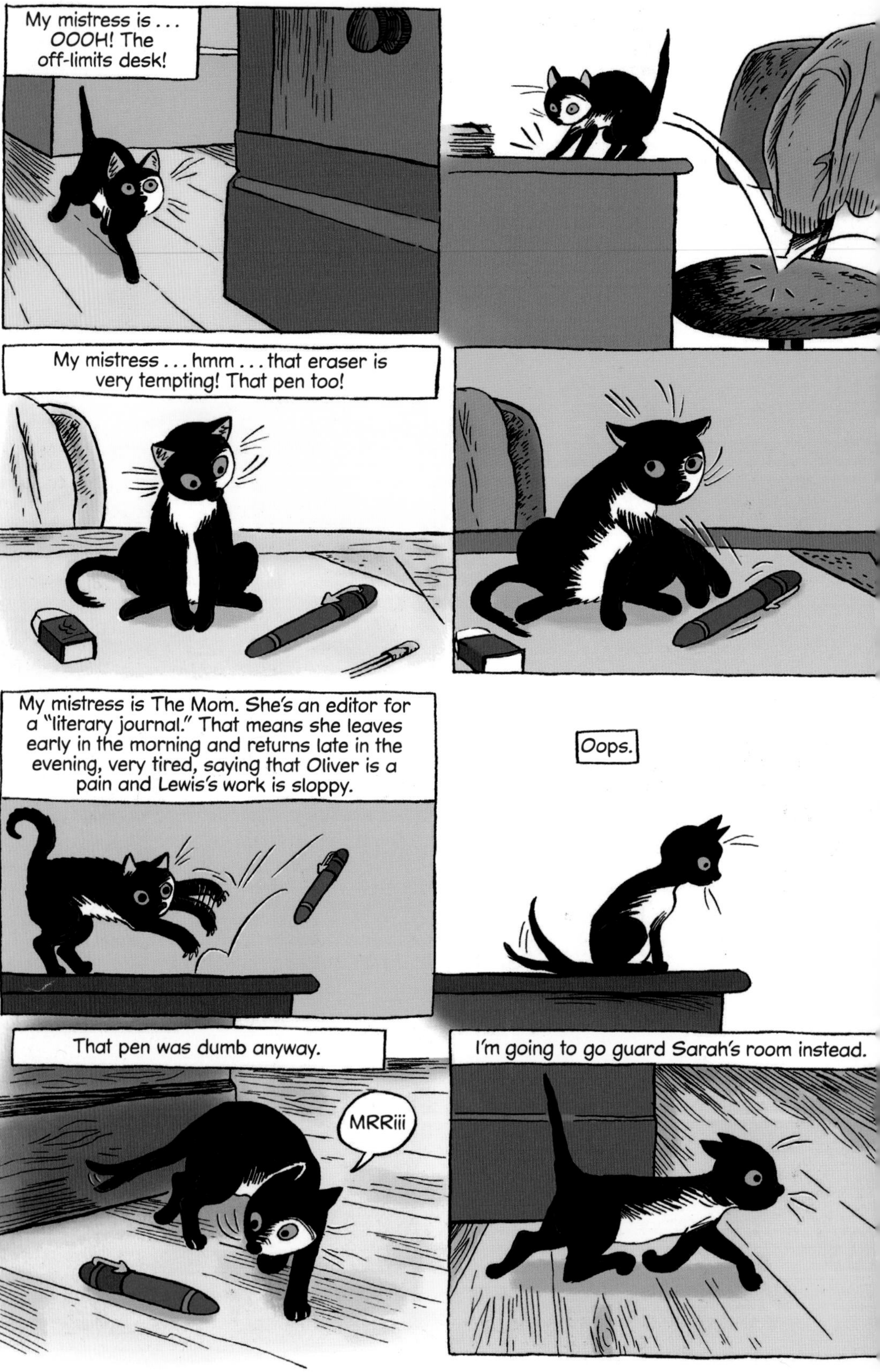

My mistress is . . . OOOH! The off-limits desk!
My mistress . . . hmm . . . that eraser is very tempting! That pen too!
My mistress is The Mom. She's an editor for a "literary journal." That means she leaves early in the morning and returns late in the evening, very tired, saying that Oliver is a pain and Lewis's work is sloppy.
Oops.
That pen was dumb anyway.
MRRiii
I'm going to go guard Sarah's room instead.

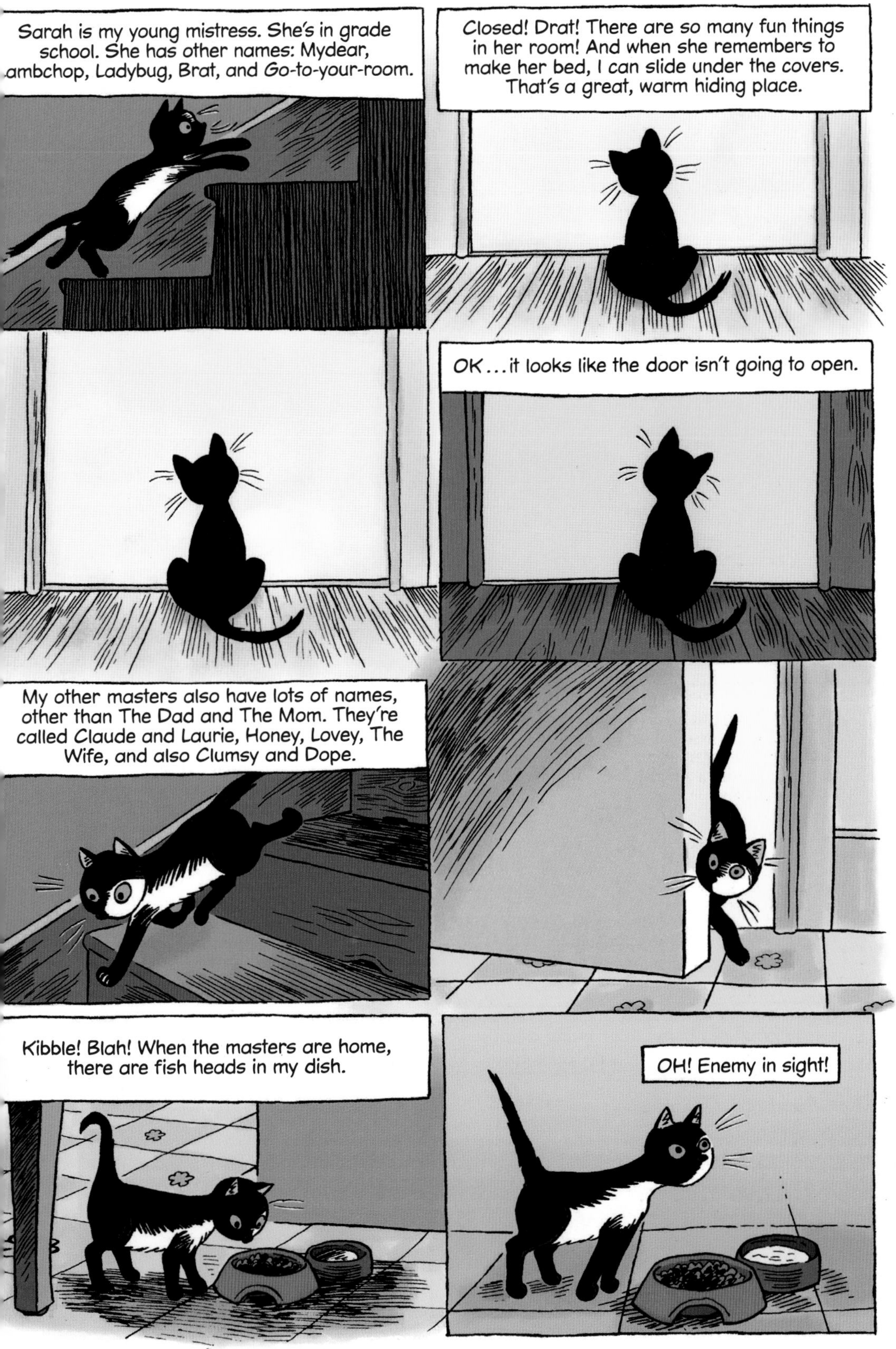
Sarah is my young mistress. She's in grade school. She has other names: Mydear, Lambchop, Ladybug, Brat, and Go-to-your-room.
Closed! Drat! There are so many fun things in her room! And when she remembers to make her bed, I can slide under the covers. That's a great, warm hiding place.
OK...it looks like the door isn't going to open.
My other masters also have lots of names, other than The Dad and The Mom. They're called Claude and Laurie, Honey, Lovey, The Wife, and also Clumsy and Dope.
Kibble! Blah! When the masters are home, there are fish heads in my dish.
OH! Enemy in sight!

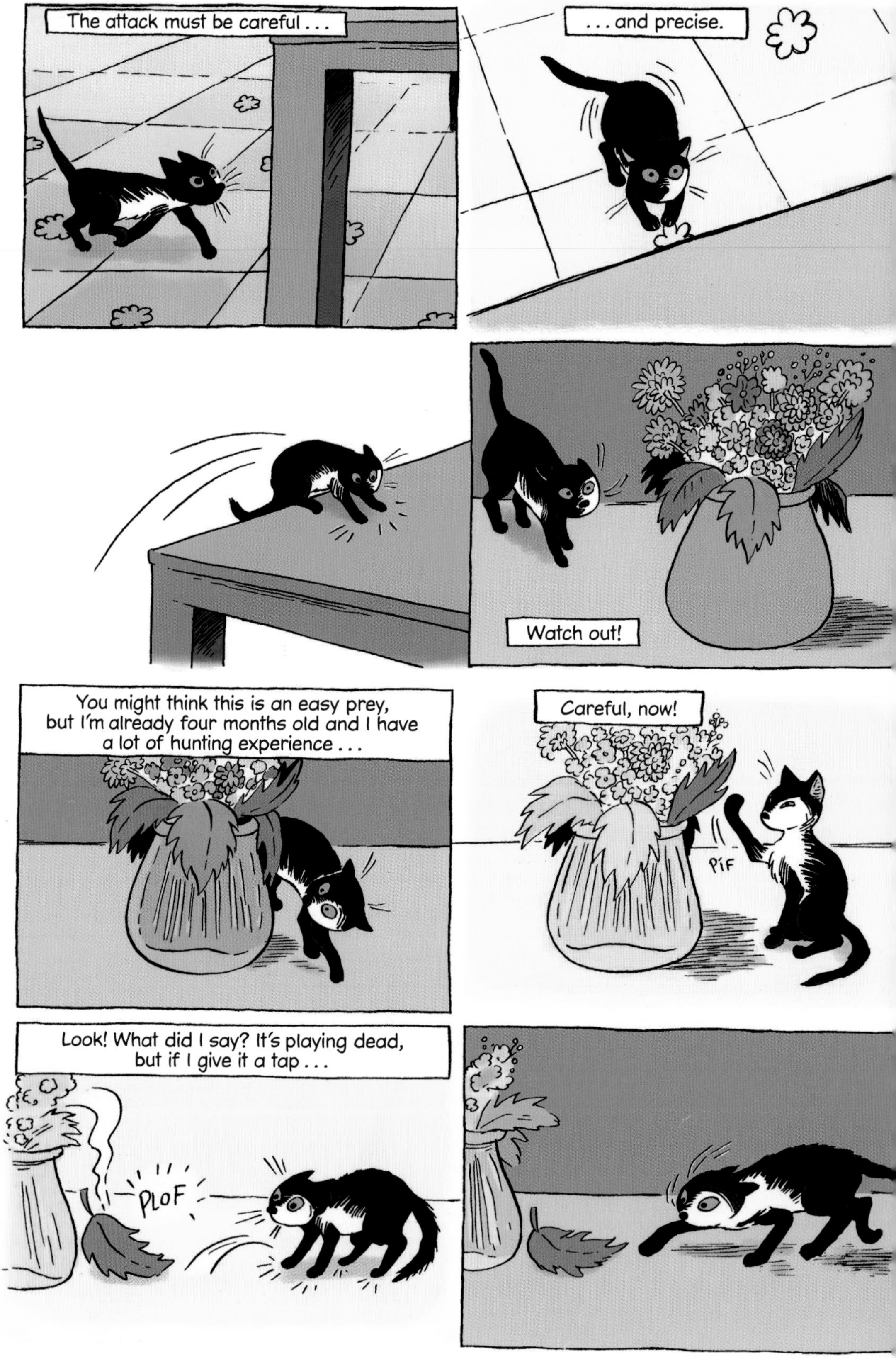
The attack must be careful . . .
. . . and precise.
Watch out!
You might think this is an easy prey, but I'm already four months old and I have a lot of hunting experience . . .
Careful, now!
PIF
Look! What did I say? It's playing dead, but if I give it a tap . . .
PLOF

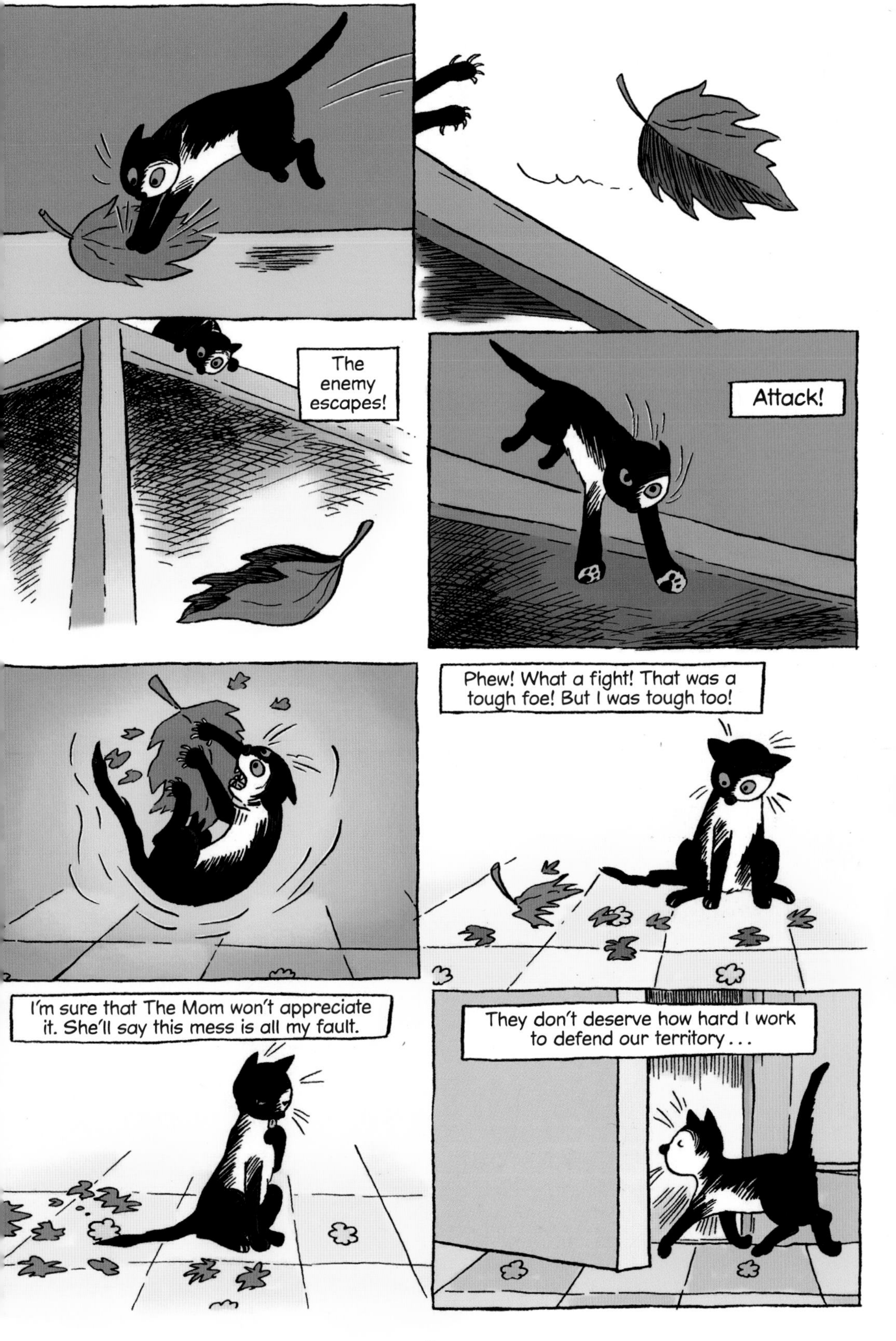
The enemy escapes!
Attack!
Phew! What a fight! That was a tough foe! But I was tough too!
I'm sure that The Mom won't appreciate it. She'll say this mess is all my fault.
They don't deserve how hard I work to defend our territory . . .

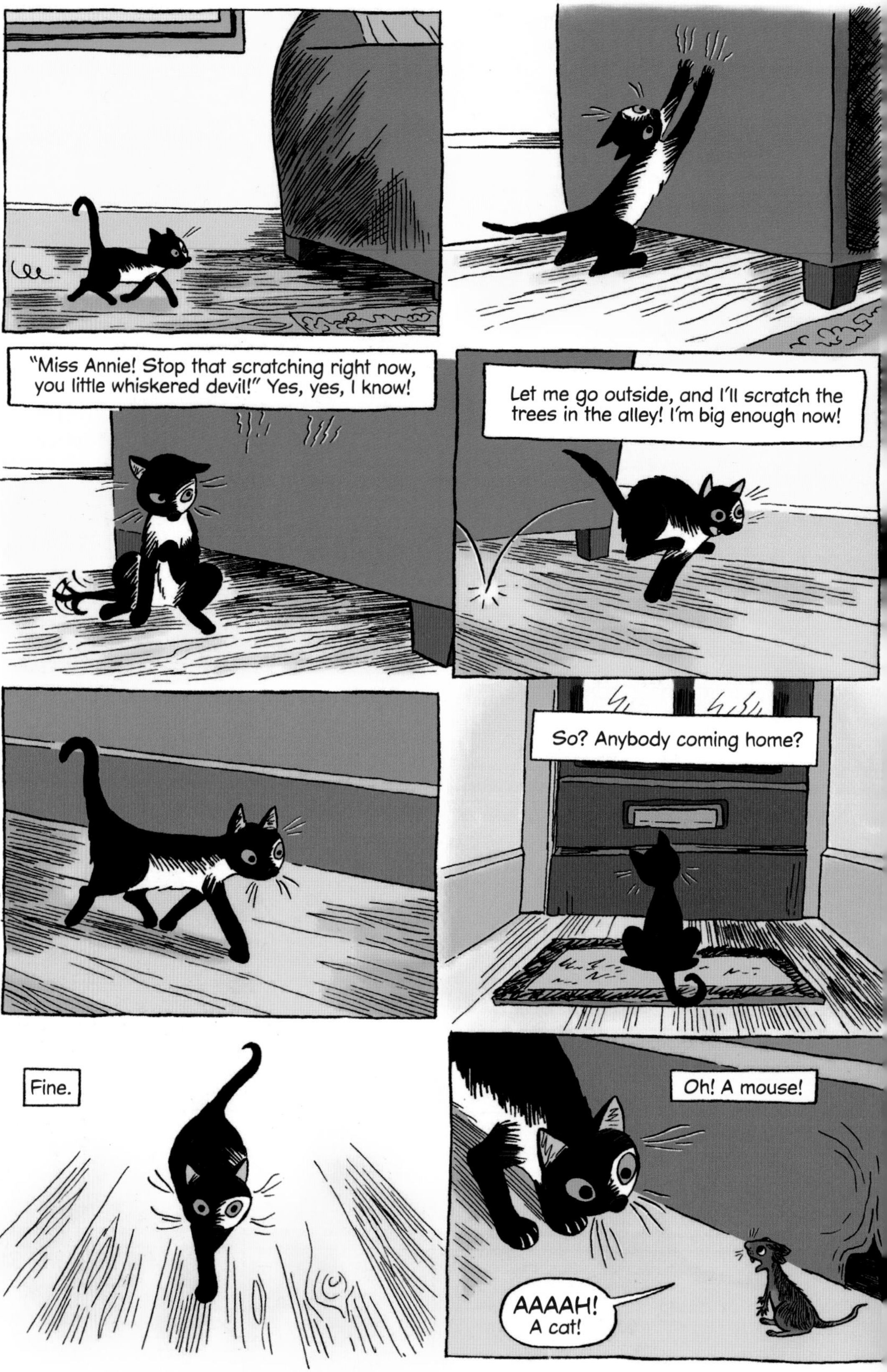
"Miss Annie! Stop that scratching right now, you little whiskered devil!" Yes, yes, I know!
Let me go outside, and I'll scratch the trees in the alley! I'm big enough now!
So? Anybody coming home?
Fine.
Oh! A mouse!
AAAAH! A cat!

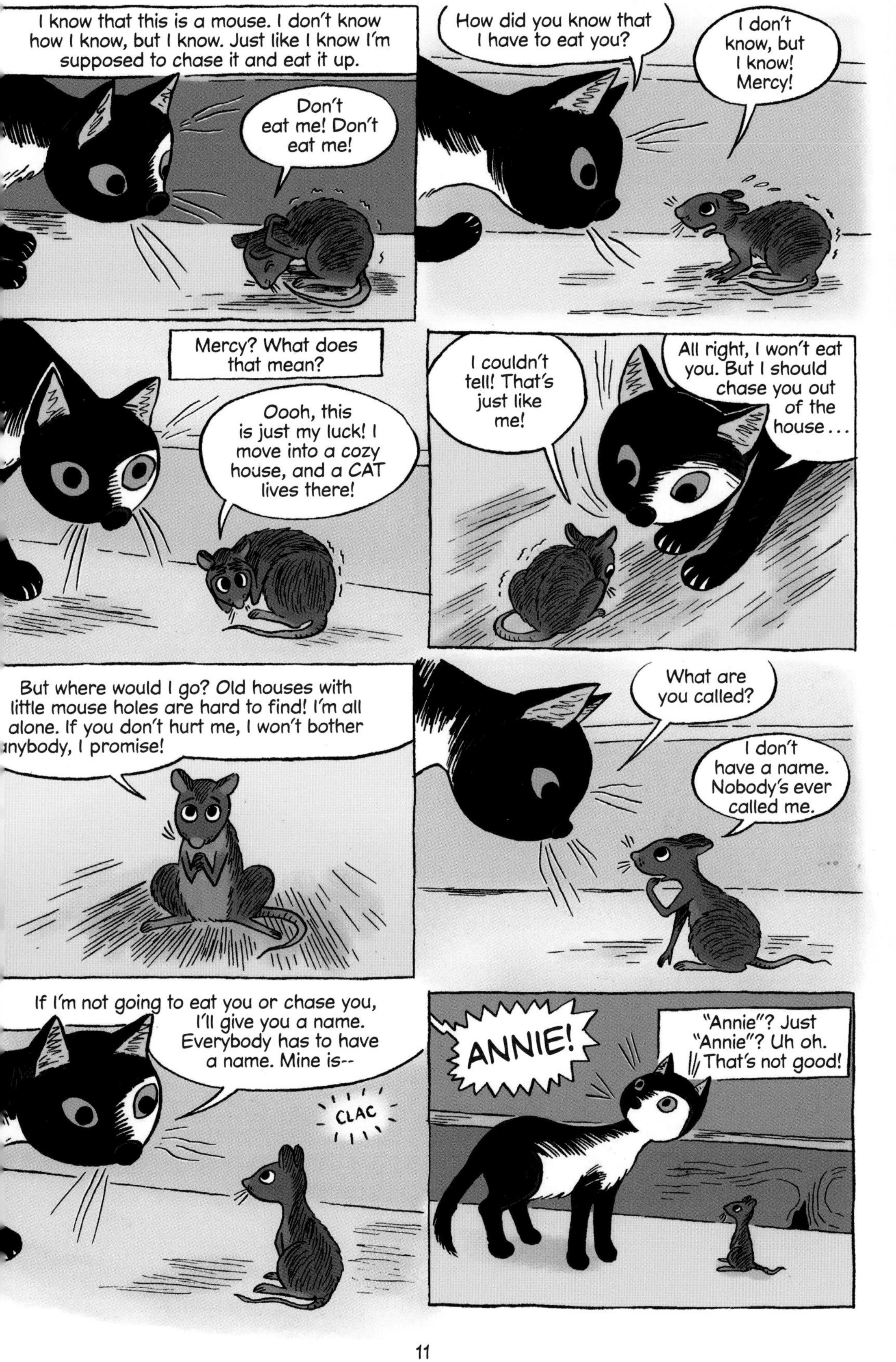
I know that this is a mouse. I don't know how I know, but I know. Just like I know I'm supposed to chase it and eat it up.
Don't eat me! Don't eat me!
How did you know that I have to eat you?
I don't know, but I know! Mercy!
Mercy? What does that mean?
Oooh, this is just my luck! I move into a cozy house, and a CAT lives there!
All right, I won't eat you. But I should chase you out of the house...
I couldn't tell! That's just like me!
But where would I go? Old houses with little mouse holes are hard to find! I'm all alone. If you don't hurt me, I won't bother anybody, I promise!
What are you called?
I don't have a name. Nobody's ever called me.
If I'm not going to eat you or chase you, I'll give you a name. Everybody has to have a name. Mine is--
CLAC
ANNIE!
"Annie"? Just "Annie"? Uh oh. That's not good!

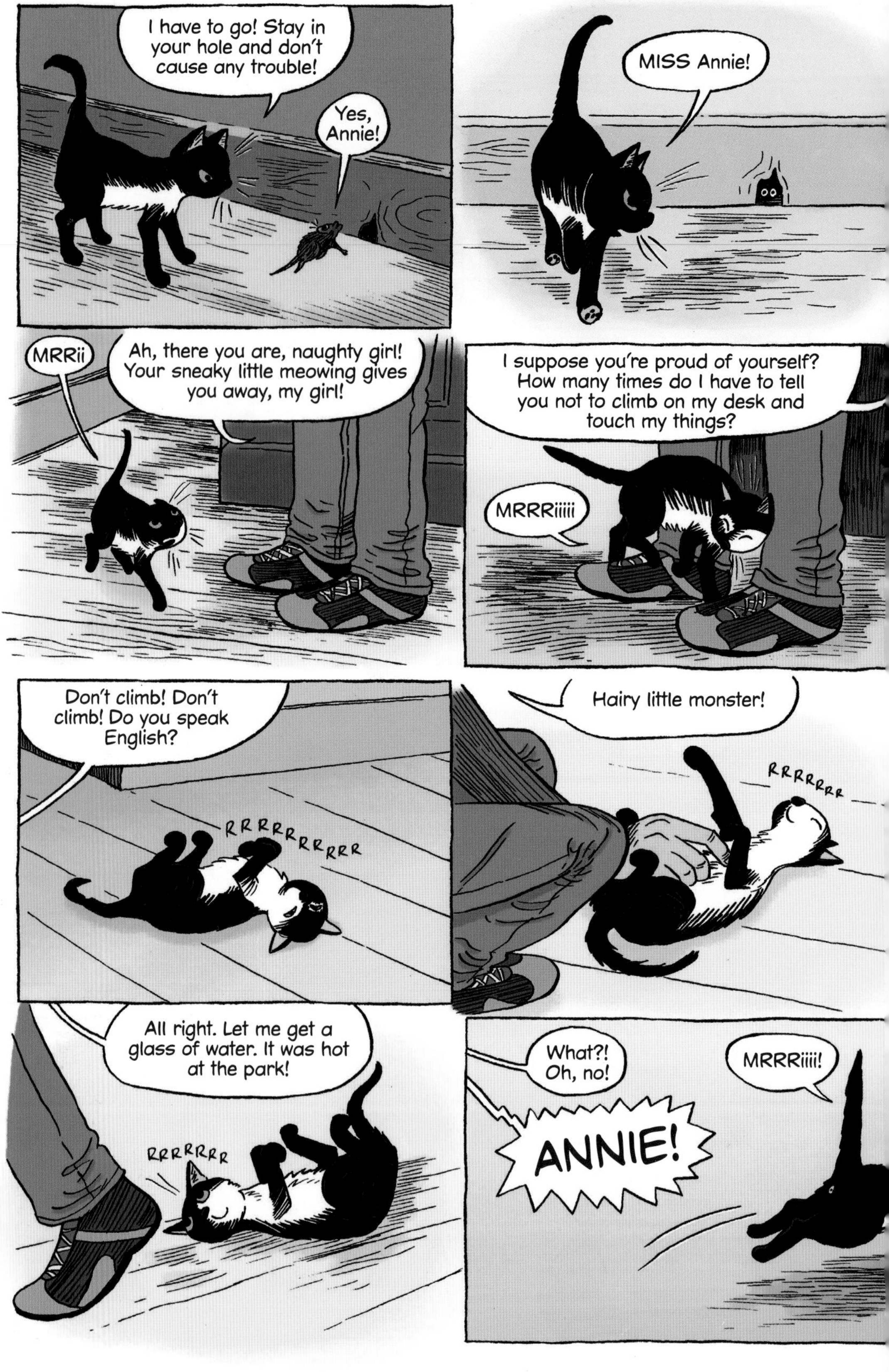
I have to go! Stay in your hole and don't cause any trouble!
Yes, Annie!
MISS Annie!
MRRii
Ah, there you are, naughty girl! Your sneaky little meowing gives you away, my girl!
I suppose you're proud of yourself? How many times do I have to tell you not to climb on my desk and touch my things?
MRRRiiiii
Don't climb! Don't climb! Do you speak English?
RRRRRRRRRR
Hairy little monster!
RRRRRRR
All right. Let me get a glass of water. It was hot at the park!
RRRRRRR
What?! Oh, no!
MRRRiiii!
ANNIE!

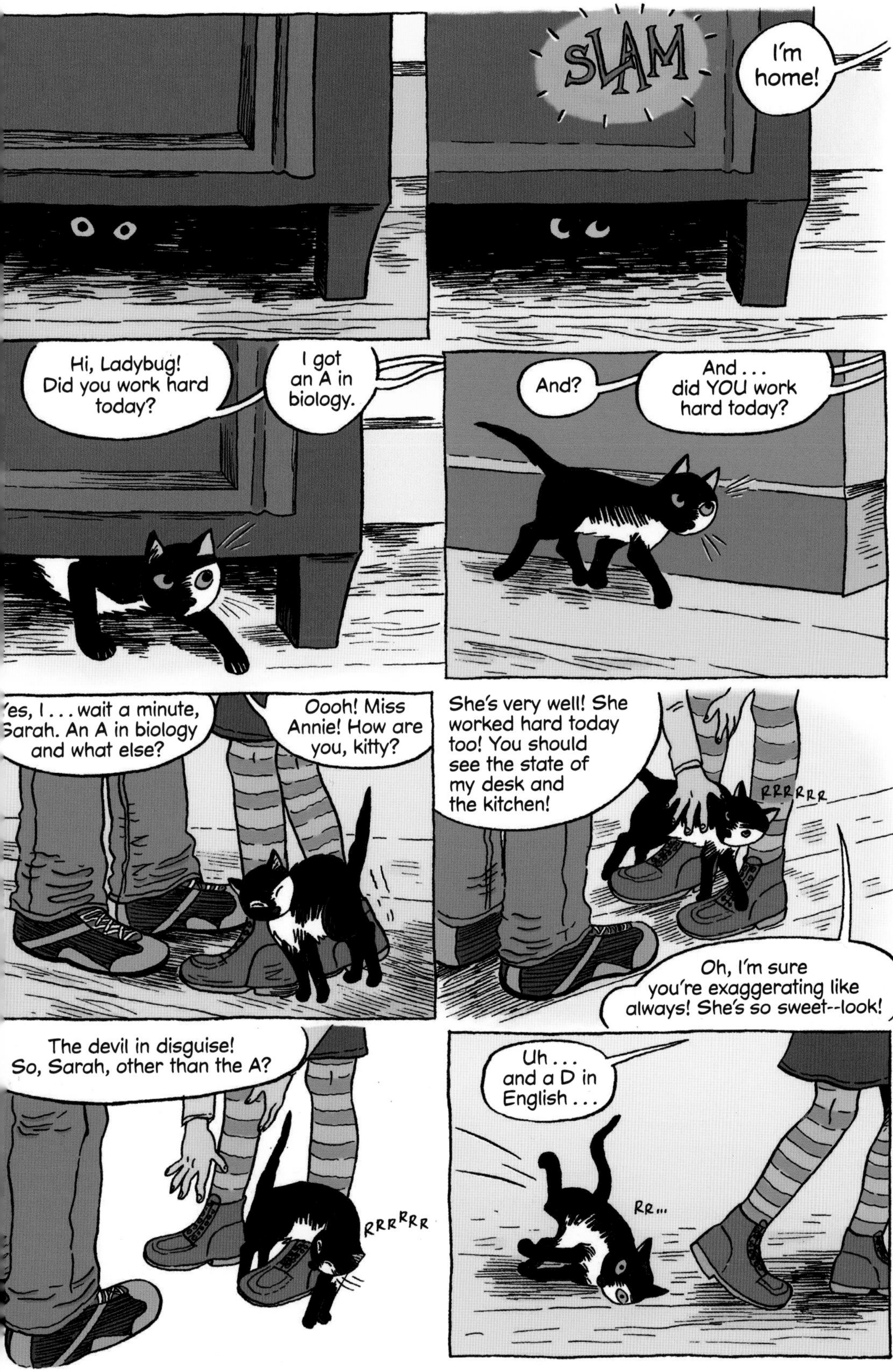
SLAM
I'm home!
Hi, Ladybug! Did you work hard today?
I got an A in biology.
And?
And . . . did YOU work hard today?
Yes, I . . . wait a minute, Sarah. An A in biology and what else?
Oooh! Miss Annie! How are you, kitty?
She's very well! She worked hard today too! You should see the state of my desk and the kitchen!
RRRRRR
Oh, I'm sure you're exaggerating like always! She's so sweet--look!
The devil in disguise! So, Sarah, other than the A?
RRRRRR
Uh . . . and a D in English . . .
RR...

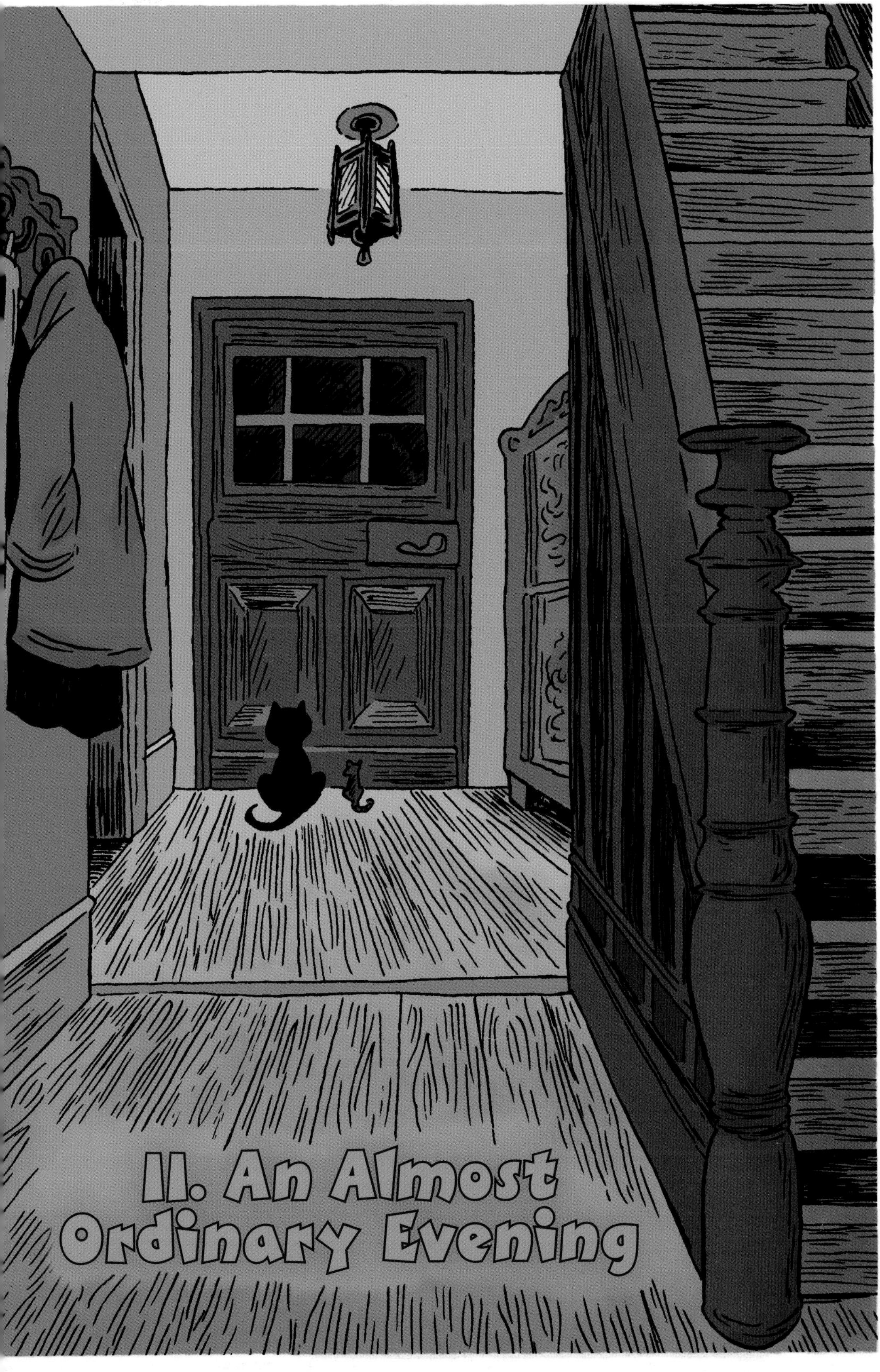
II. An Almost
Ordinary Evening

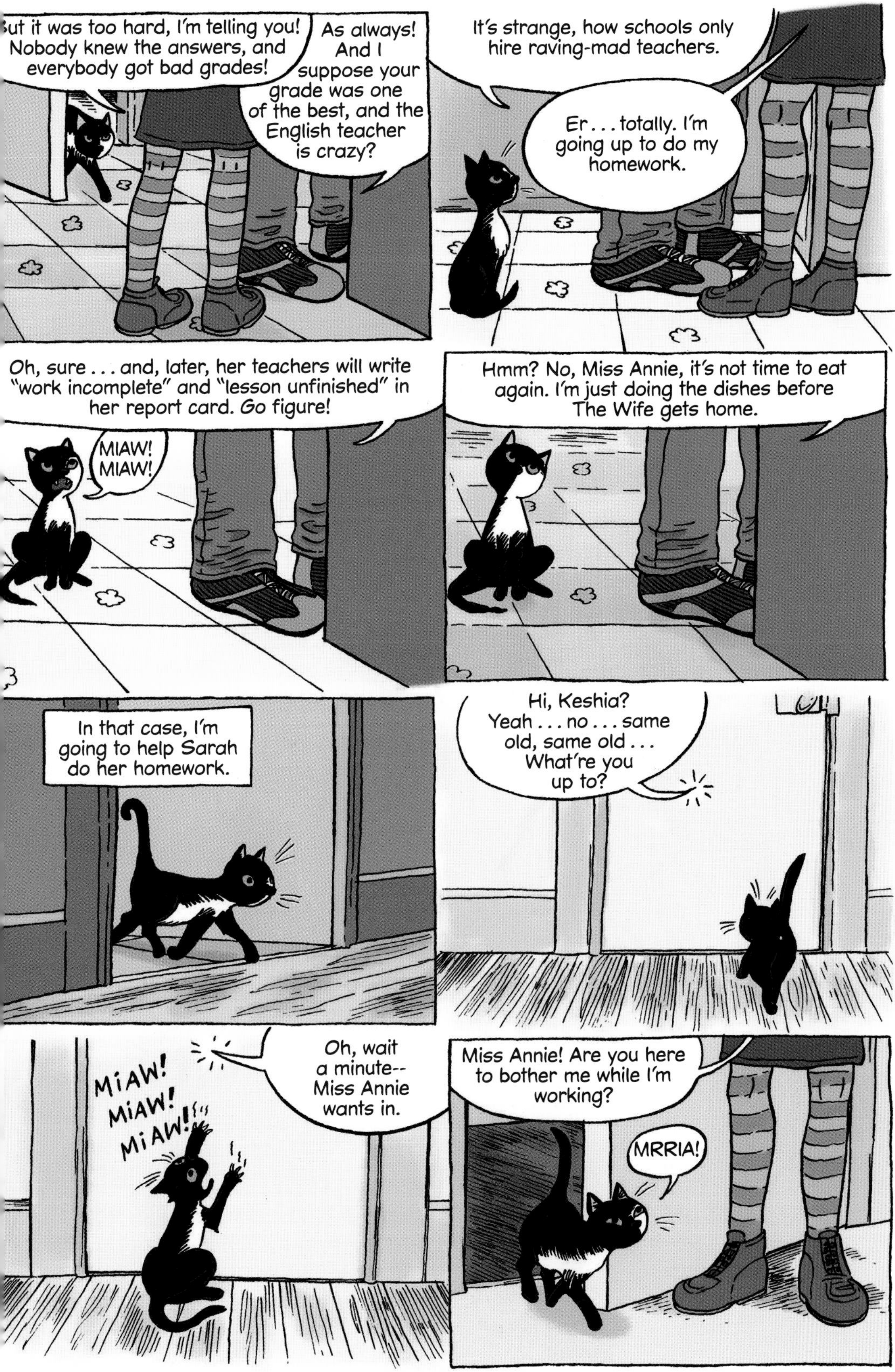
But it was too hard, I'm telling you! Nobody knew the answers, and everybody got bad grades!
As always! And I suppose your grade was one of the best, and the English teacher is crazy?
It's strange, how schools only hire raving-mad teachers.
Er . . . totally. I'm going up to do my homework.
Oh, sure . . . and, later, her teachers will write "work incomplete" and "lesson unfinished" in her report card. Go figure!
MIAW! MIAW!
Hmm? No, Miss Annie, it's not time to eat again. I'm just doing the dishes before The Wife gets home.
In that case, I'm going to help Sarah do her homework.
Hi, Keshia? Yeah . . . no . . . same old, same old . . . What're you up to?
MIAW! MIAW! MIAW!
Oh, wait a minute-- Miss Annie wants in.
Miss Annie! Are you here to bother me while I'm working?
MRRIA!

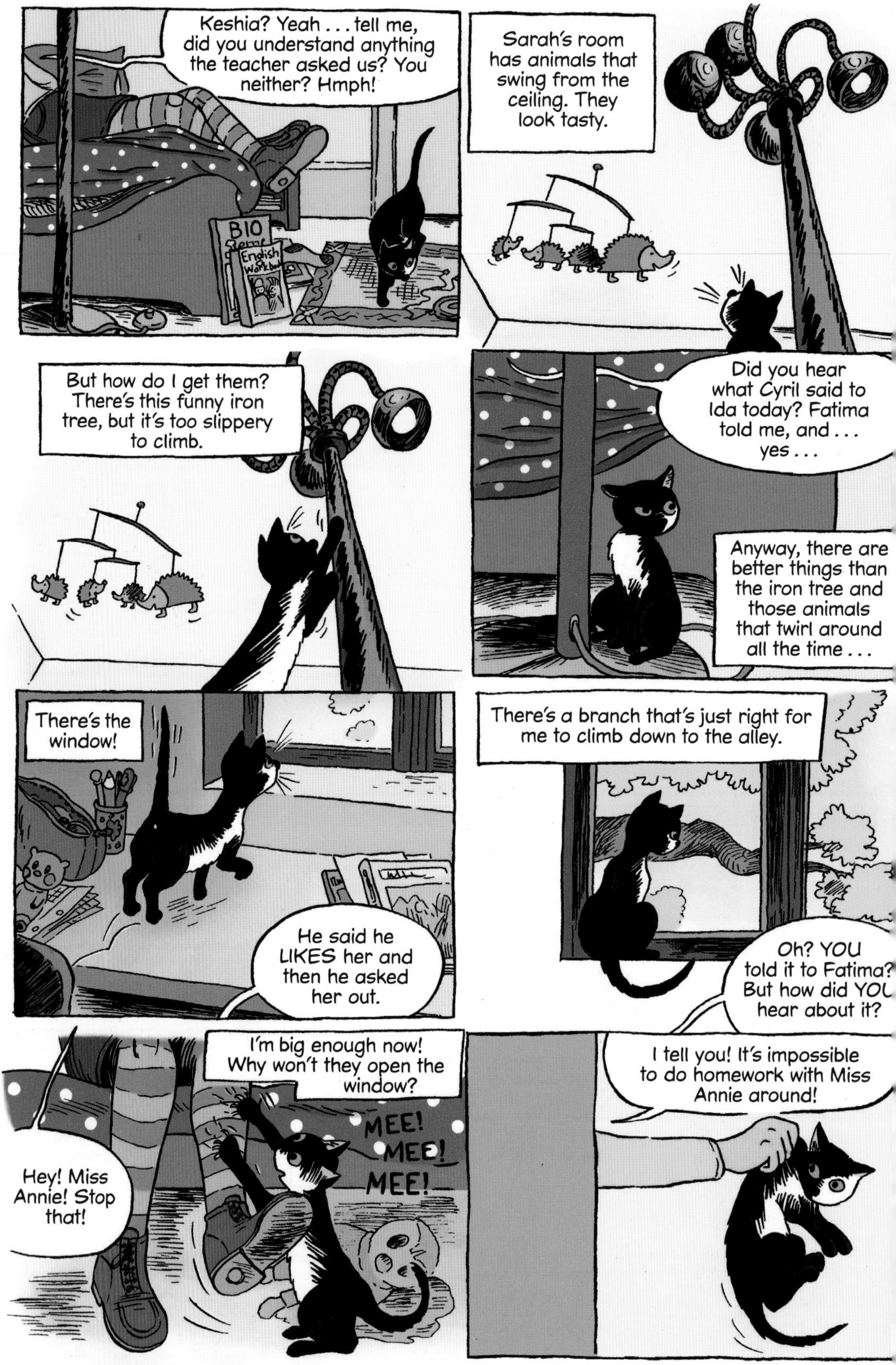
Keshia? Yeah . . . tell me, did you understand anything the teacher asked us? You neither? Hmph!
BIO
English Workbook
Sarah's room has animals that swing from the ceiling. They look tasty.
But how do I get them? There's this funny iron tree, but it's too slippery to climb.
Did you hear what Cyril said to Ida today? Fatima told me, and . . . yes . . .
Anyway, there are better things than the iron tree and those animals that twirl around all the time . . .
There's the window!
He said he LIKES her and then he asked her out.
There's a branch that's just right for me to climb down to the alley.
Oh? YOU told it to Fatima? But how did YOU hear about it?
I'm big enough now! Why won't they open the window?
Hey! Miss Annie! Stop that!
MEE! MEE! MEE!
I tell you! It's impossible to do homework with Miss Annie around!

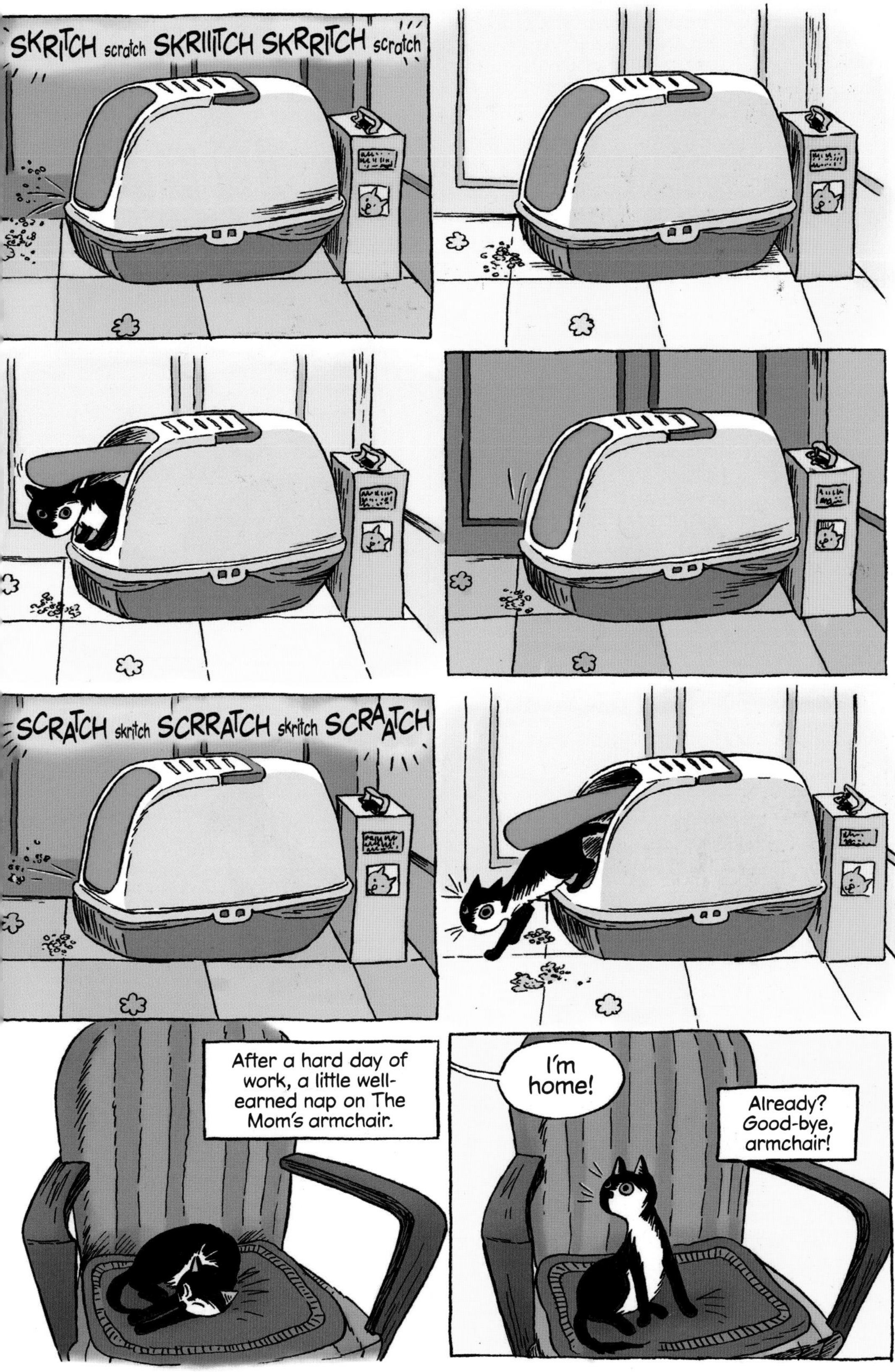
SKRITCH scratch SKRIIITCH SKRRITCH scratch
SCRATCH skritch SCRRATCH skritch SCRAATCH
After a hard day of work, a little well-earned nap on The Mom's armchair.
I'm home!
Already? Good-bye, armchair!

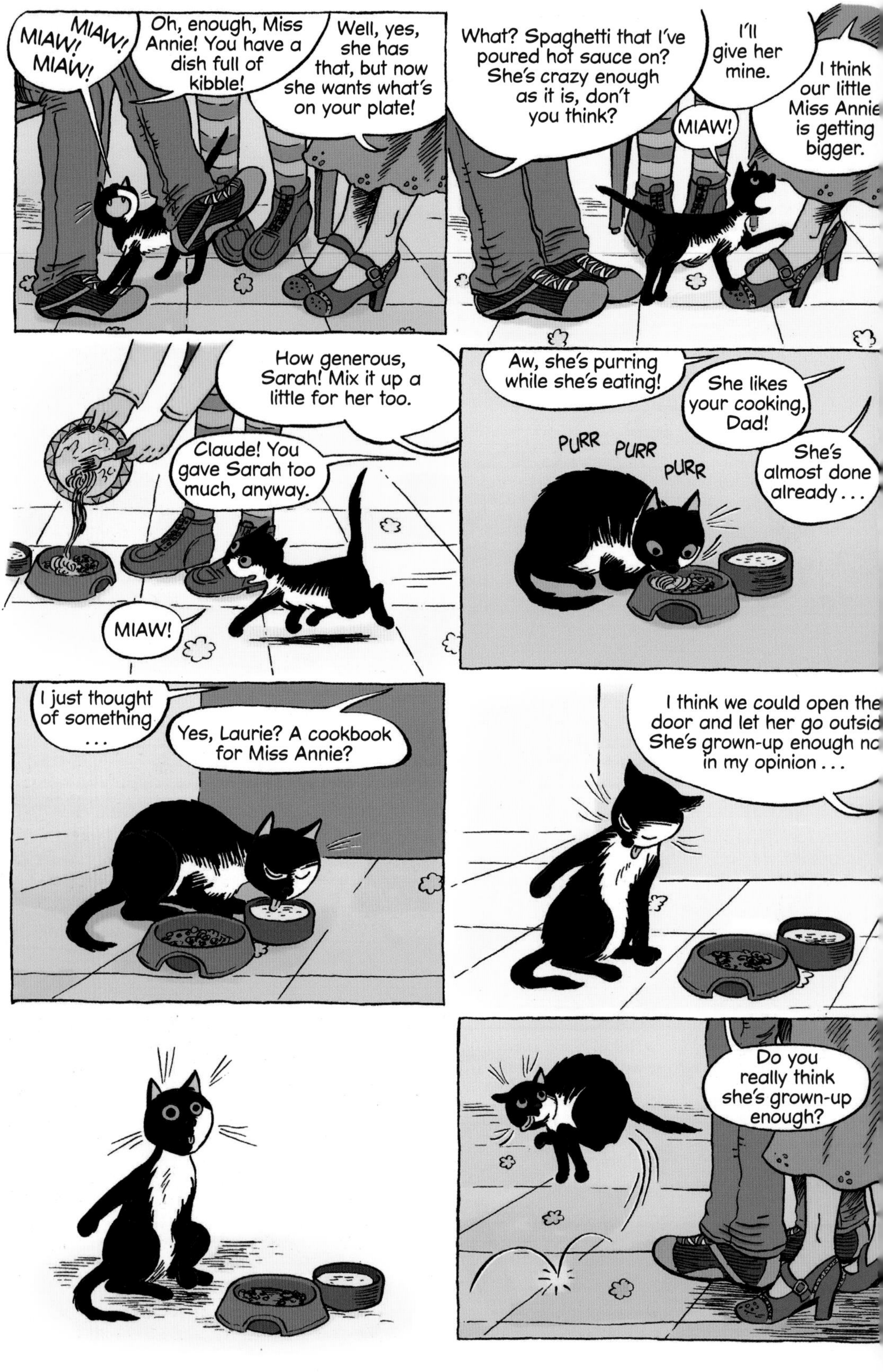
MIAW! MIAW! MIAW!
Oh, enough, Miss Annie! You have a dish full of kibble!
Well, yes, she has that, but now she wants what's on your plate!
What? Spaghetti that I've poured hot sauce on? She's crazy enough as it is, don't you think?
I'll give her mine.
MIAW!
I think our little Miss Annie is getting bigger.
How generous, Sarah! Mix it up a little for her too.
Claude! You gave Sarah too much, anyway.
MIAW!
Aw, she's purring while she's eating!
She likes your cooking, Dad!
PURR PURR PURR
She's almost done already . . .
I just thought of something . . .
Yes, Laurie? A cookbook for Miss Annie?
I think we could open the door and let her go outsid She's grown-up enough no in my opinion . . .
Do you really think she's grown-up enough?

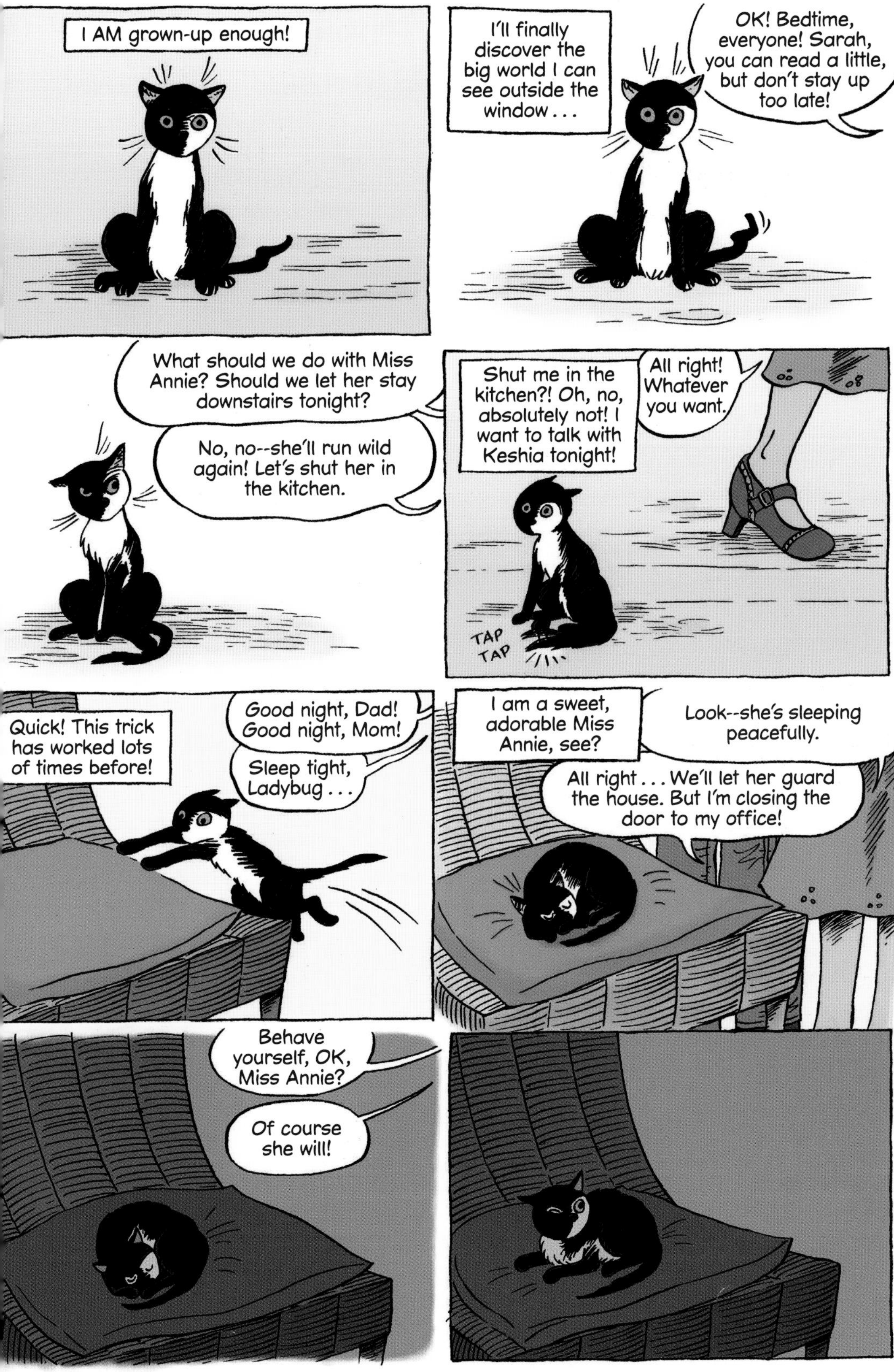
I AM grown-up enough!
I'll finally discover the big world I can see outside the window . . .
OK! Bedtime, everyone! Sarah, you can read a little, but don't stay up too late!
What should we do with Miss Annie? Should we let her stay downstairs tonight?
No, no--she'll run wild again! Let's shut her in the kitchen.
Shut me in the kitchen?! Oh, no, absolutely not! I want to talk with Keshia tonight!
All right! Whatever you want.
TAP TAP
Quick! This trick has worked lots of times before!
Good night, Dad! Good night, Mom!
Sleep tight, Ladybug . . .
I am a sweet, adorable Miss Annie, see?
Look--she's sleeping peacefully.
All right . . . We'll let her guard the house. But I'm closing the door to my office!
Behave yourself, OK, Miss Annie?
Of course she will!

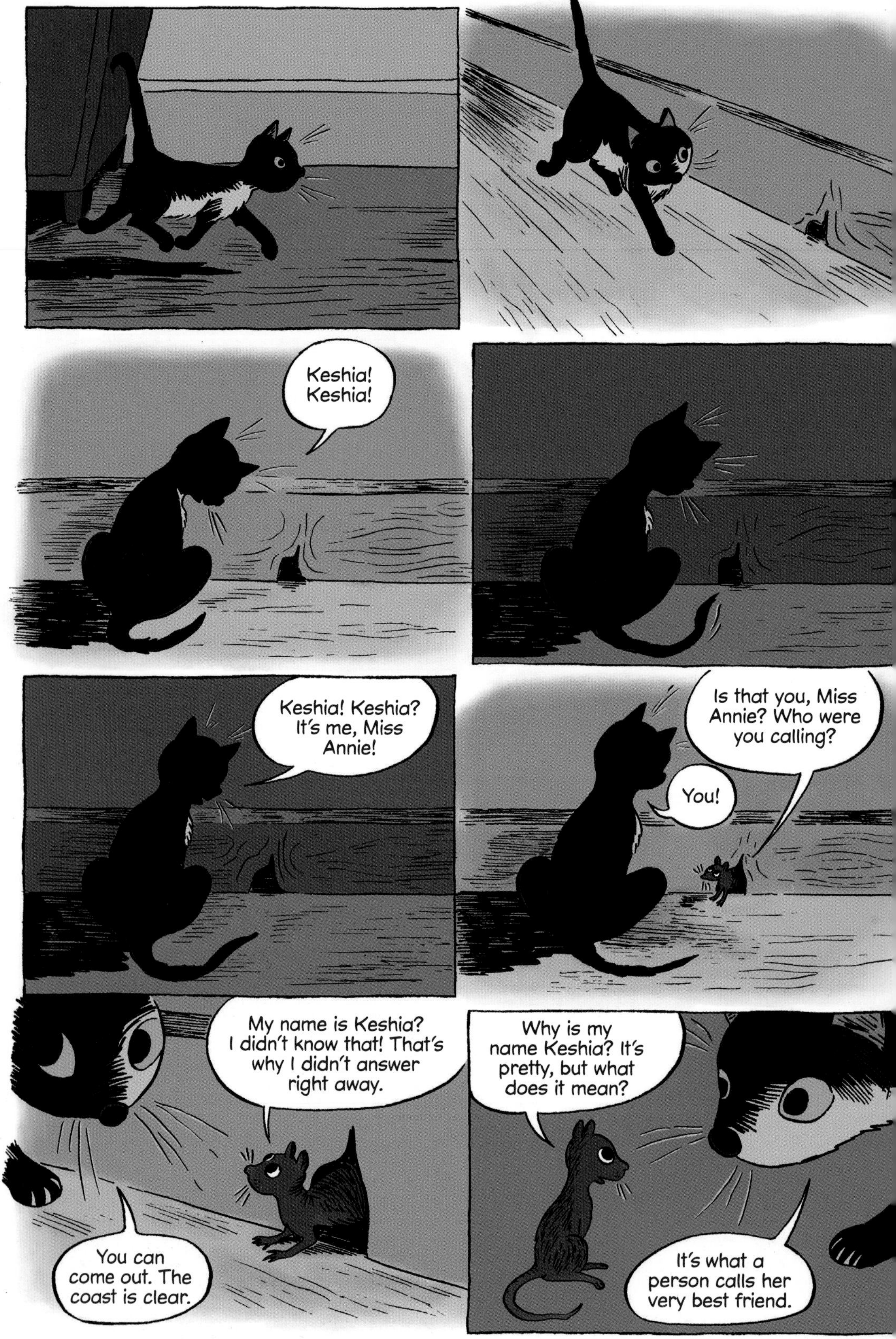
Keshia! Keshia!
Keshia! Keshia? It's me, Miss Annie!
Is that you, Miss Annie? Who were you calling?
You!
My name is Keshia? I didn't know that! That's why I didn't answer right away.
You can come out. The coast is clear.
Why is my name Keshia? It's pretty, but what does it mean?
It's what a person calls her very best friend.

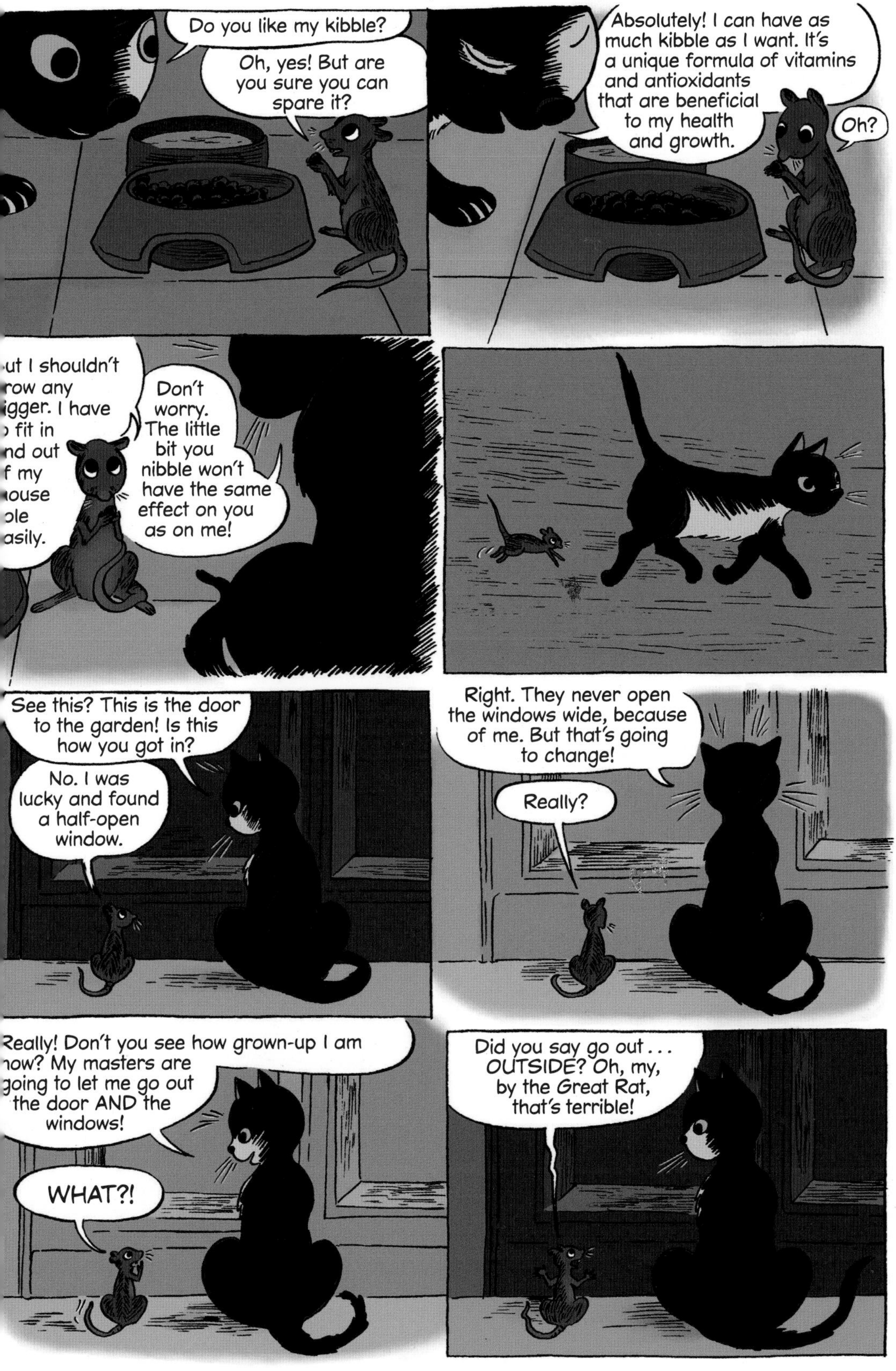

Do you like my kibble?
Oh, yes! But are you sure you can spare it?
Absolutely! I can have as much kibble as I want. It's a unique formula of vitamins and antioxidants that are beneficial to my health and growth.
Oh?
ut I shouldn't row any igger. I have fit in nd out f my ouse ole asily.
Don't worry. The little bit you nibble won't have the same effect on you as on me!
See this? This is the door to the garden! Is this how you got in?
No. I was lucky and found a half-open window.
Right. They never open the windows wide, because of me. But that's going to change!
Really?
eally! Don't you see how grown-up I am ow? My masters are oing to let me go out the door AND the windows!
WHAT?!
Did you say go out . . . OUTSIDE? Oh, my, by the Great Rat, that's terrible!

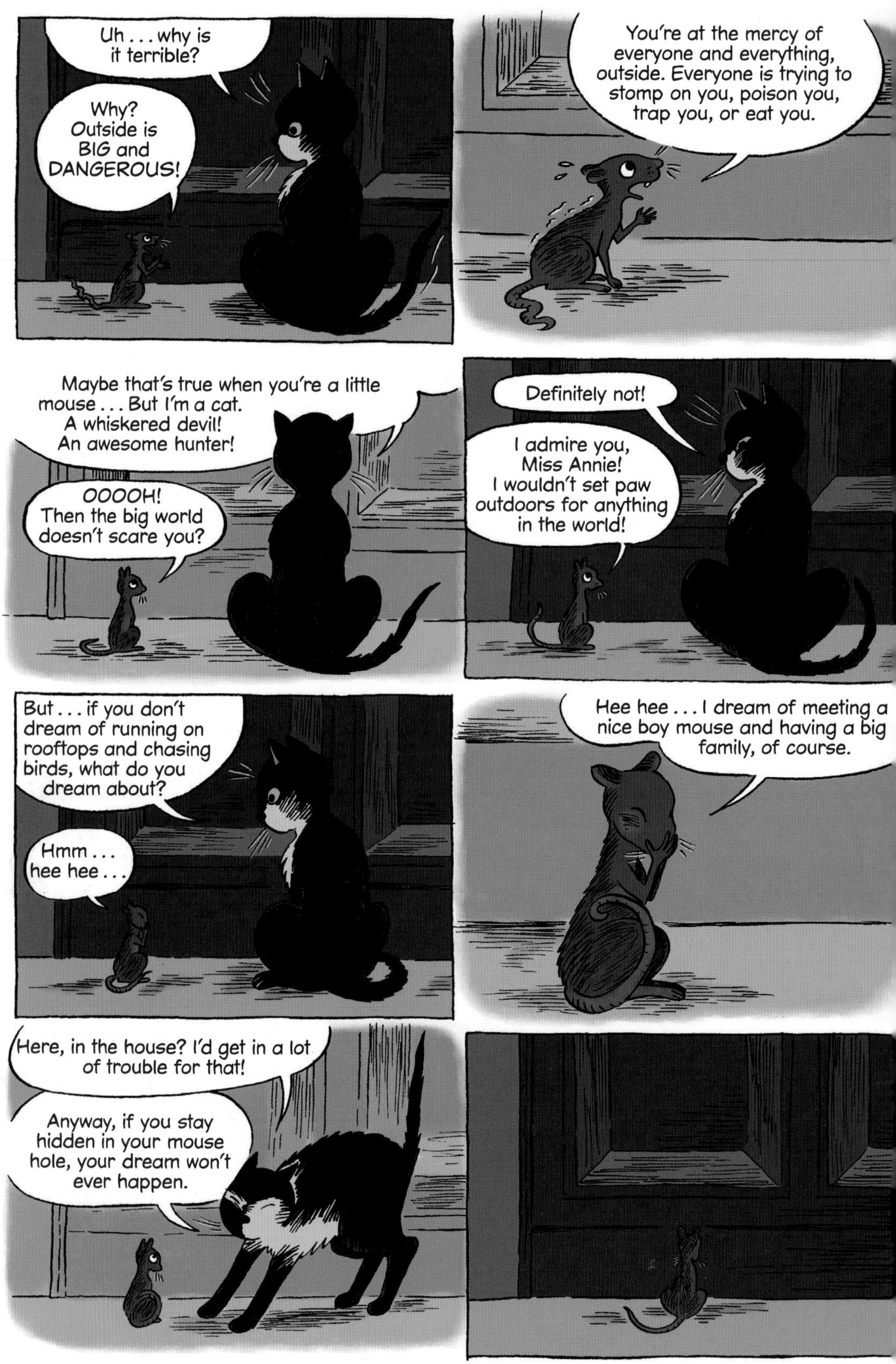
Uh . . . why is it terrible?
Why? Outside is BIG and DANGEROUS!
You're at the mercy of everyone and everything, outside. Everyone is trying to stomp on you, poison you, trap you, or eat you.
Maybe that's true when you're a little mouse . . . But I'm a cat. A whiskered devil! An awesome hunter!
OOOOH! Then the big world doesn't scare you?
Definitely not!
I admire you, Miss Annie! I wouldn't set paw outdoors for anything in the world!
But . . . if you don't dream of running on rooftops and chasing birds, what do you dream about?
Hmm . . . hee hee . . .
Hee hee . . . I dream of meeting a nice boy mouse and having a big family, of course.
Here, in the house? I'd get in a lot of trouble for that!
Anyway, if you stay hidden in your mouse hole, your dream won't ever happen.

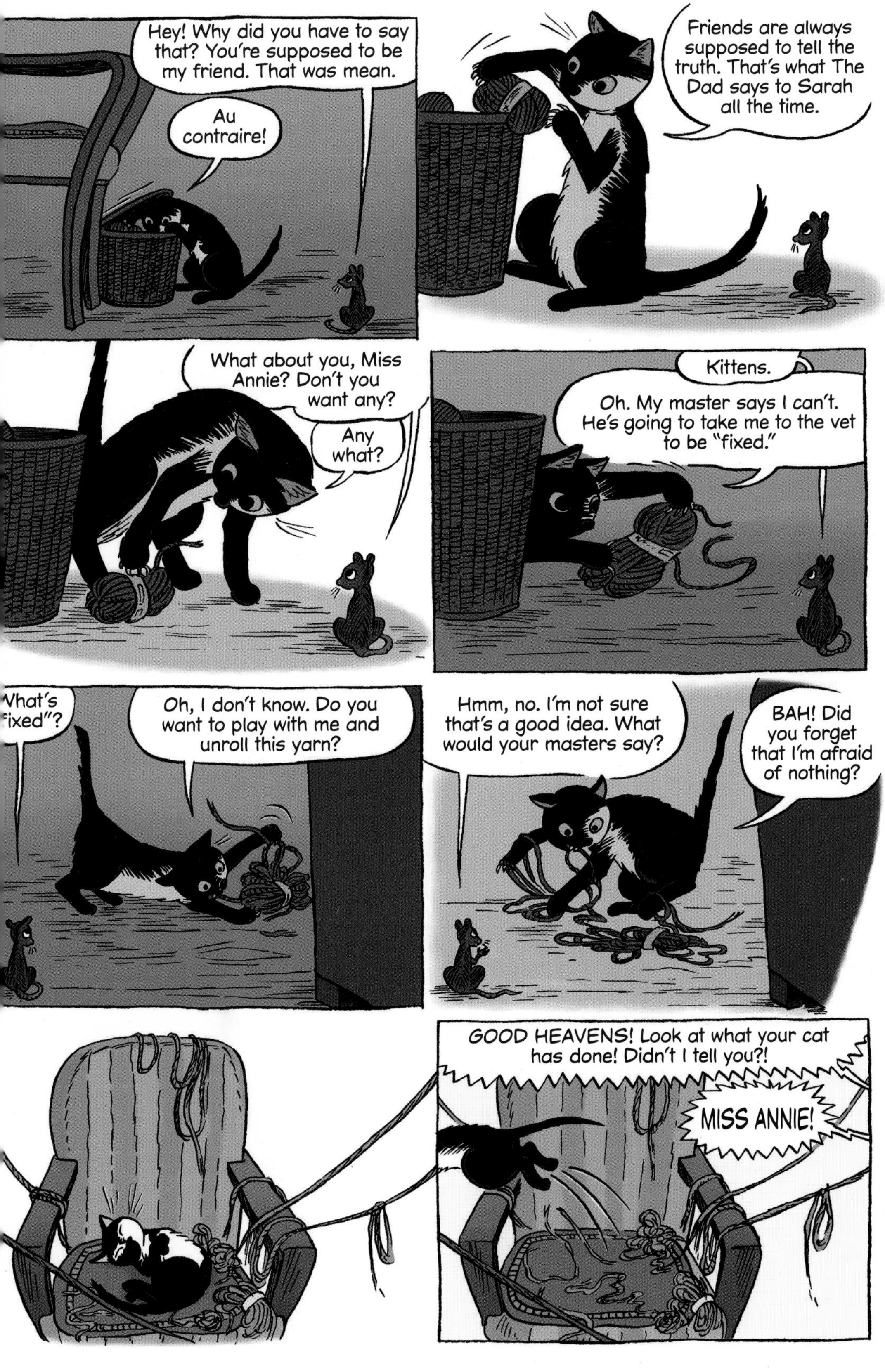
Hey! Why did you have to say that? You're supposed to be my friend. That was mean.
Au contraire!
Friends are always supposed to tell the truth. That's what The Dad says to Sarah all the time.
What about you, Miss Annie? Don't you want any?
Any what?
Kittens.
Oh. My master says I can't. He's going to take me to the vet to be "fixed."
What's fixed"?
Oh, I don't know. Do you want to play with me and unroll this yarn?
Hmm, no. I'm not sure that's a good idea. What would your masters say?
BAH! Did you forget that I'm afraid of nothing?
GOOD HEAVENS! Look at what your cat has done! Didn't I tell you?!
MISS ANNIE!

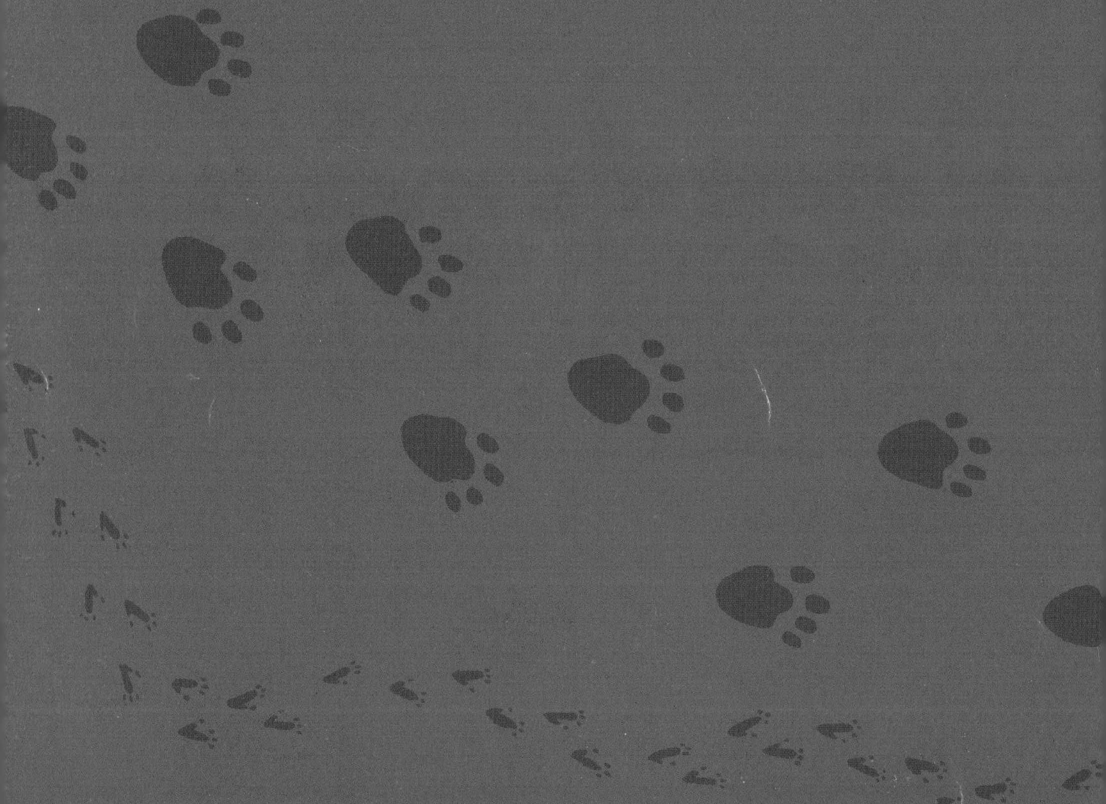

III. Freedom

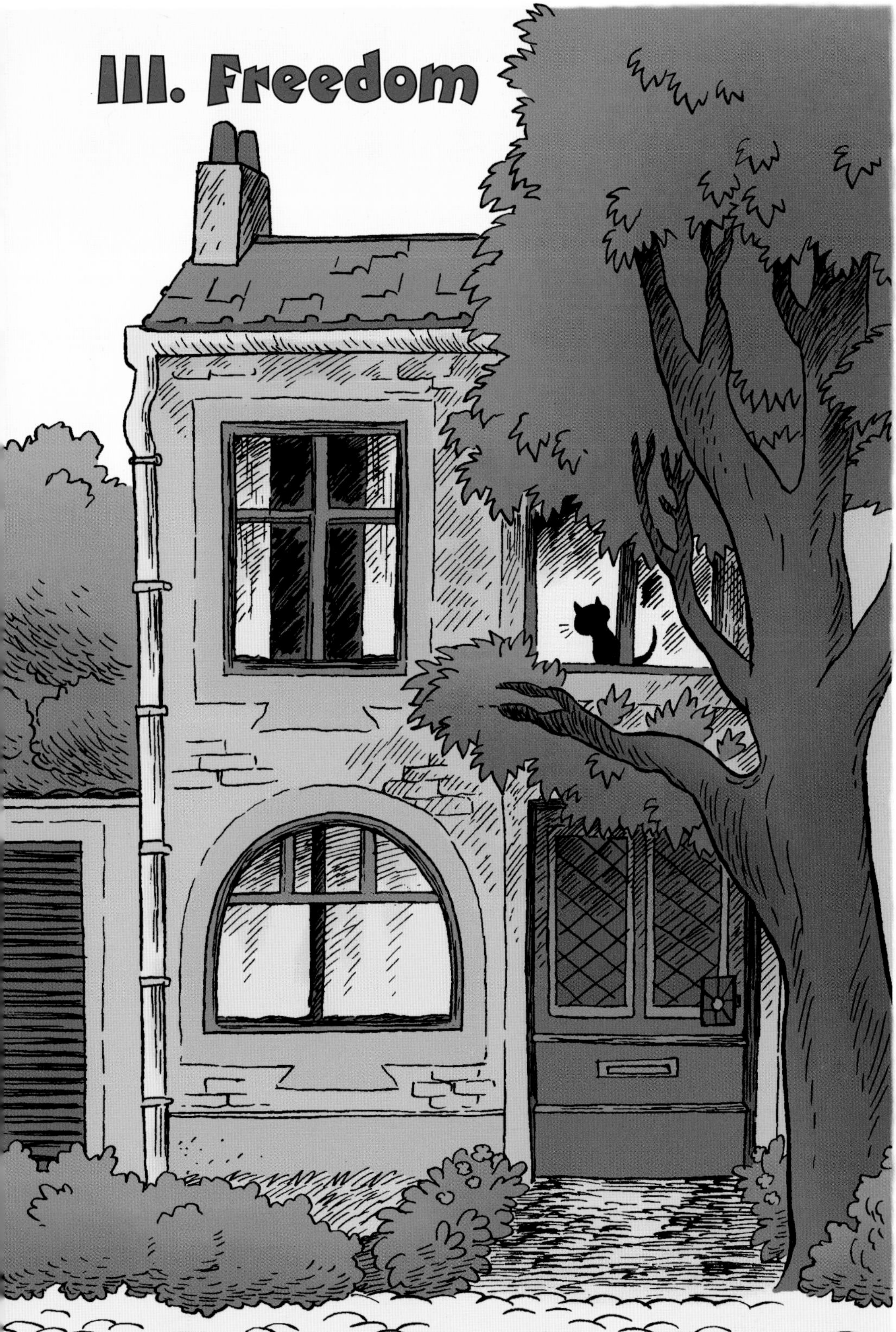

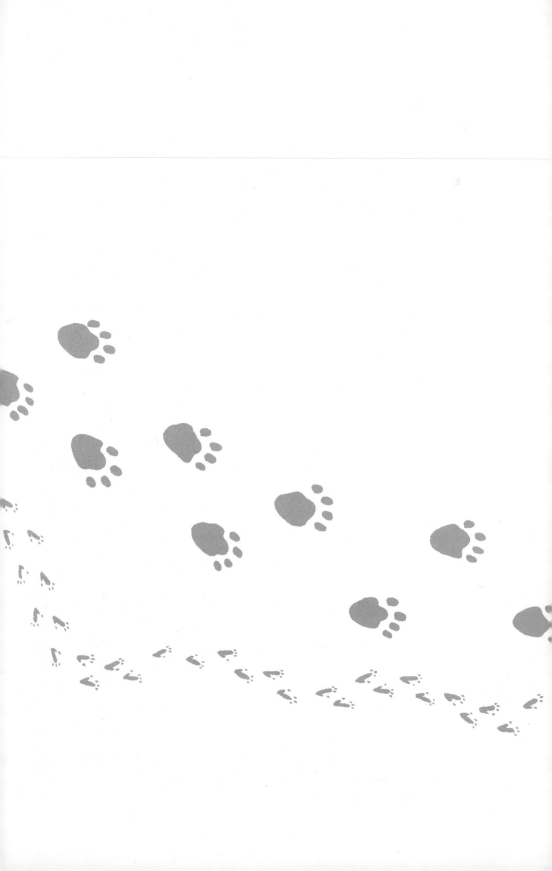

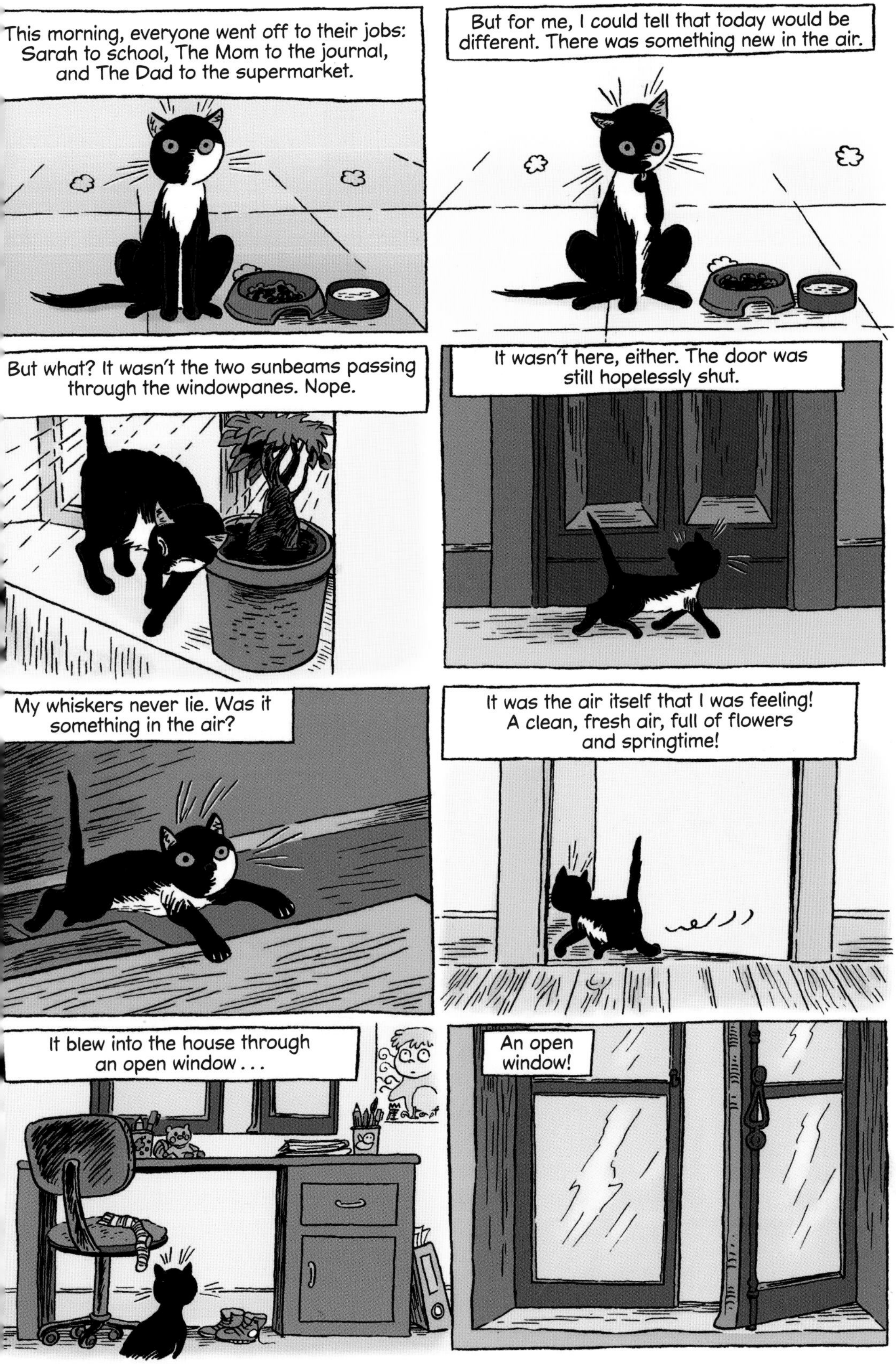
This morning, everyone went off to their jobs: Sarah to school, The Mom to the journal, and The Dad to the supermarket.
But for me, I could tell that today would be different. There was something new in the air.
But what? It wasn't the two sunbeams passing through the windowpanes. Nope.
It wasn't here, either. The door was still hopelessly shut.
My whiskers never lie. Was it something in the air?
It was the air itself that I was feeling! A clean, fresh air, full of flowers and springtime!
It blew into the house through an open window . . .
An open window!

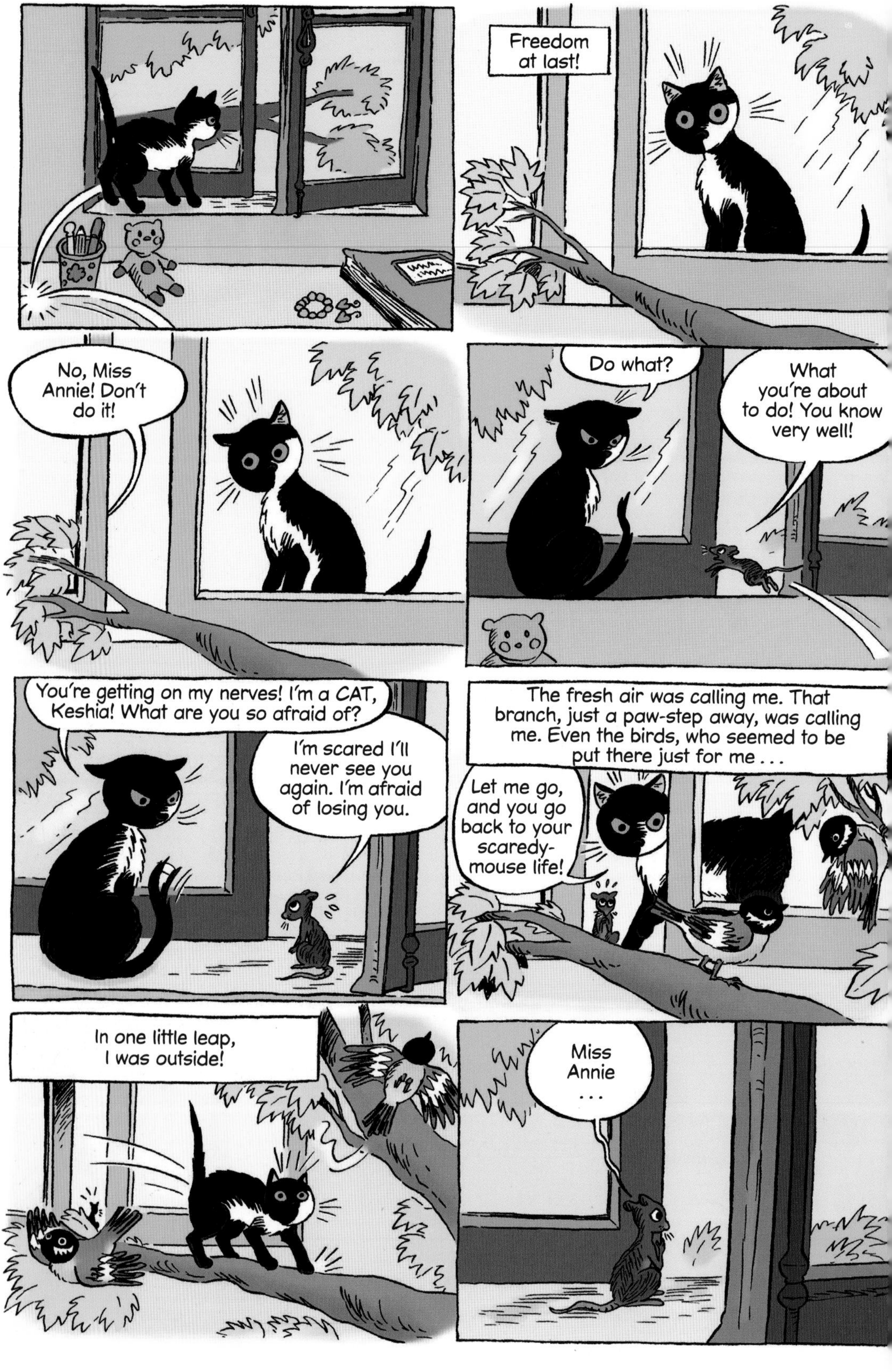
Freedom at last!
No, Miss Annie! Don't do it!
Do what?
What you're about to do! You know very well!
You're getting on my nerves! I'm a CAT, Keshia! What are you so afraid of?
I'm scared I'll never see you again. I'm afraid of losing you.
The fresh air was calling me. That branch, just a paw-step away, was calling me. Even the birds, who seemed to be put there just for me . . .
Let me go, and you go back to your scaredy-mouse life!
In one little leap, I was outside!
Miss Annie . . .

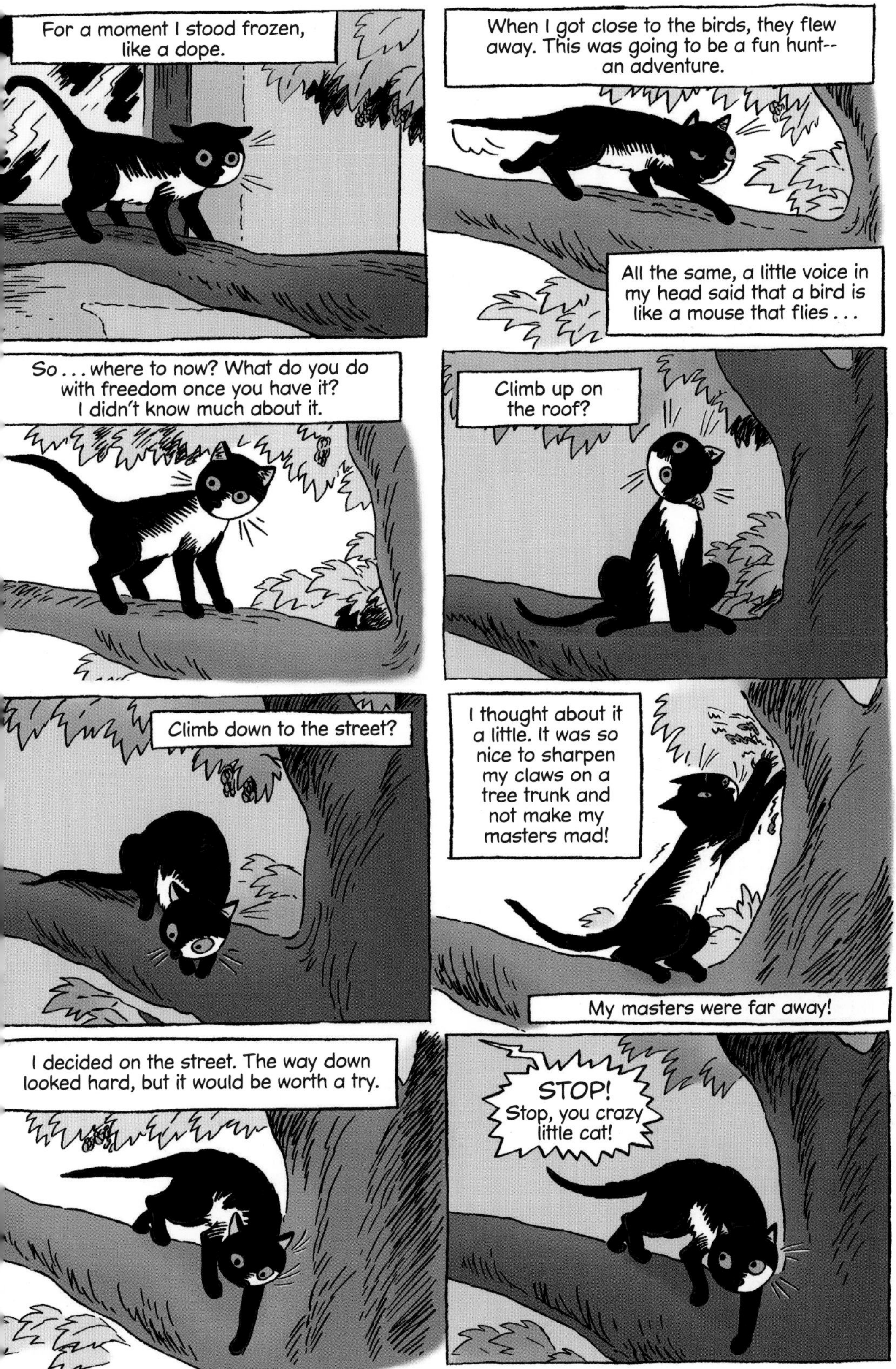
For a moment I stood frozen, like a dope.
When I got close to the birds, they flew away. This was going to be a fun hunt-- an adventure.
All the same, a little voice in my head said that a bird is like a mouse that flies . . .
So . . . where to now? What do you do with freedom once you have it? I didn't know much about it.
Climb up on the roof?
Climb down to the street?
I thought about it a little. It was so nice to sharpen my claws on a tree trunk and not make my masters mad!
My masters were far away!
I decided on the street. The way down looked hard, but it would be worth a try.
STOP! Stop, you crazy little cat!

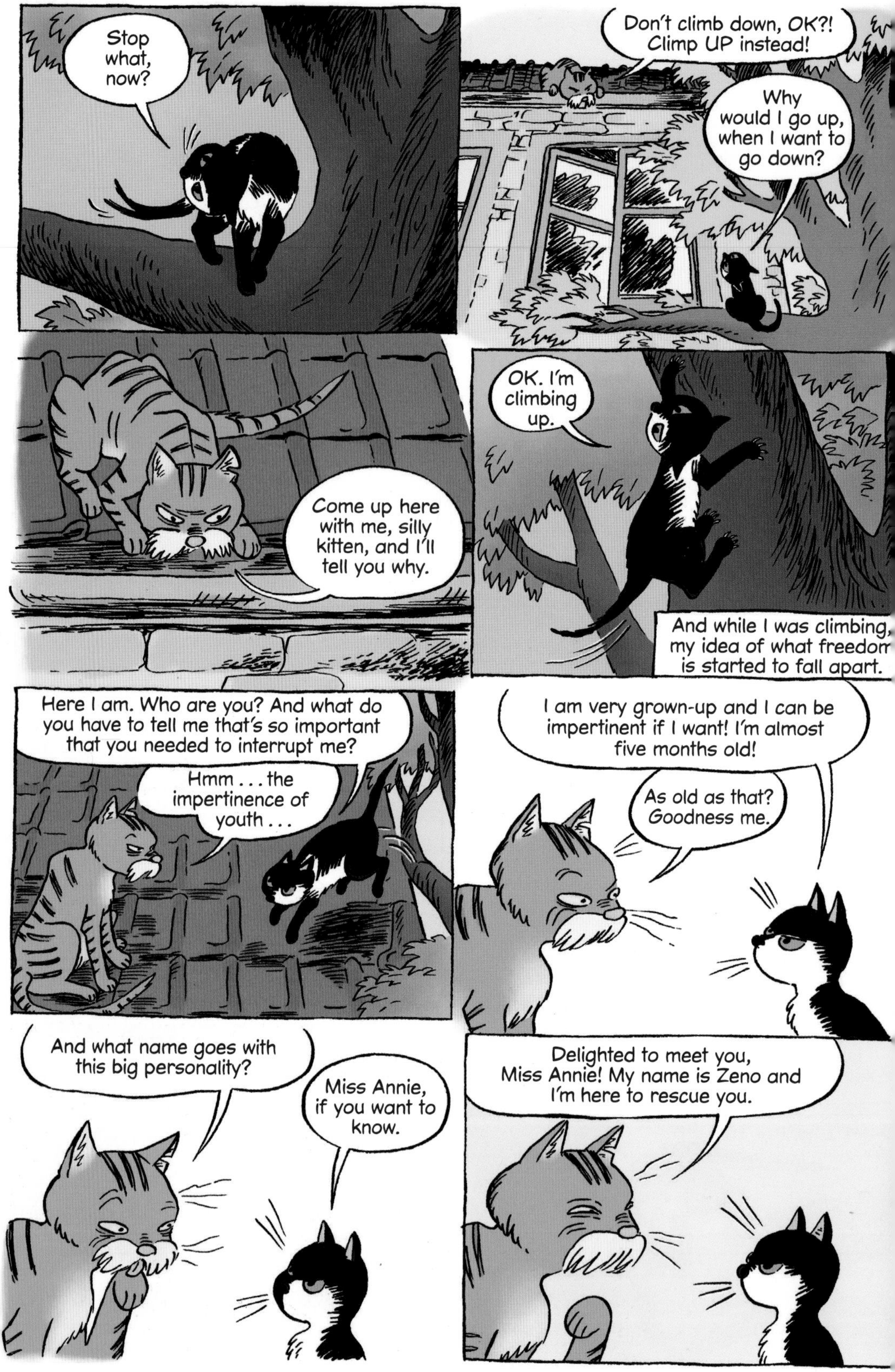
Stop what, now?
Don't climb down, OK?! Climp UP instead!
Why would I go up, when I want to go down?
Come up here with me, silly kitten, and I'll tell you why.
OK. I'm climbing up.
And while I was climbing, my idea of what freedom is started to fall apart.
Here I am. Who are you? And what do you have to tell me that's so important that you needed to interrupt me?
Hmm . . . the impertinence of youth . . .
I am very grown-up and I can be impertinent if I want! I'm almost five months old!
As old as that? Goodness me.
And what name goes with this big personality?
Miss Annie, if you want to know.
Delighted to meet you, Miss Annie! My name is Zeno and I'm here to rescue you.

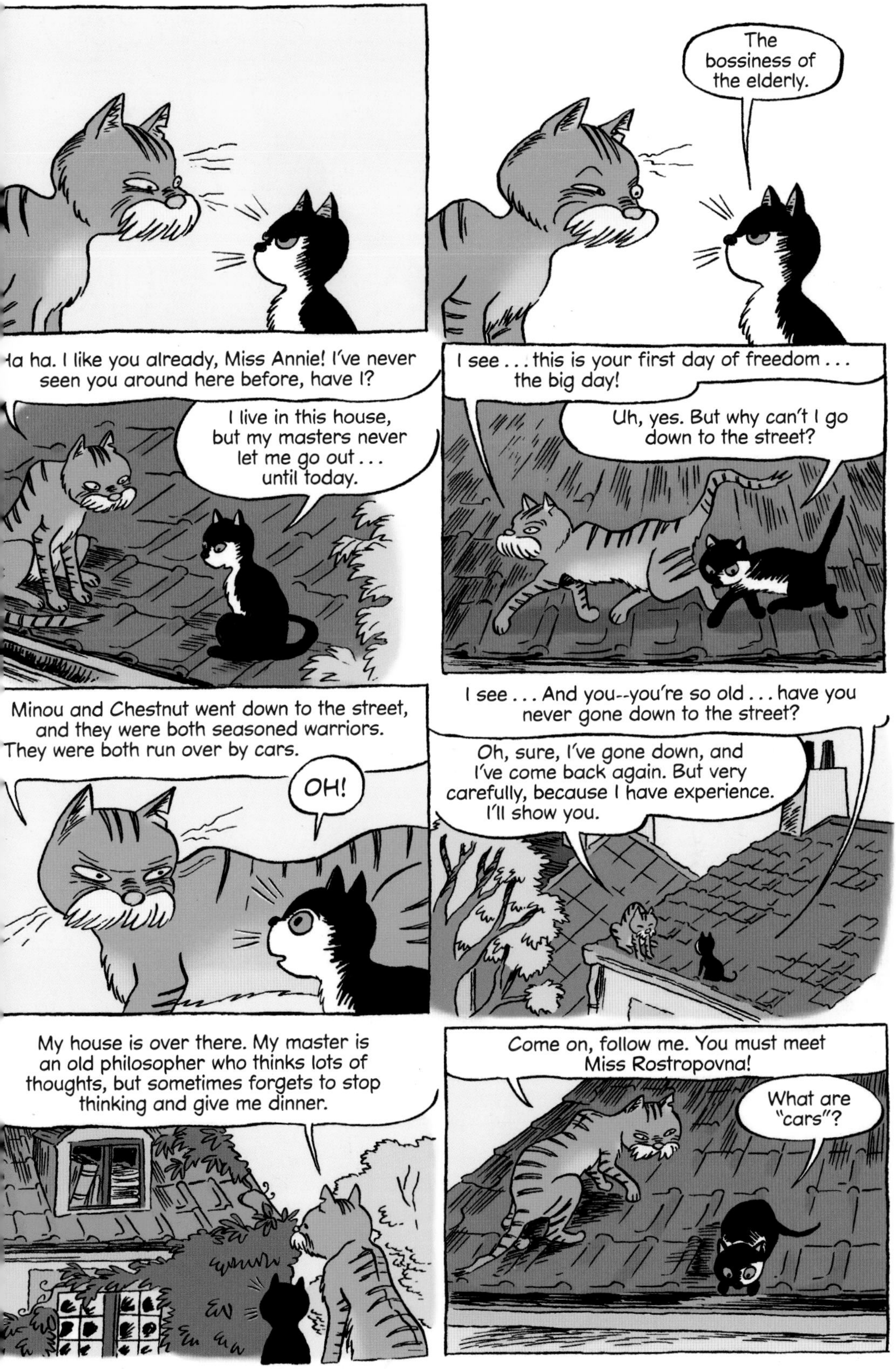
The bossiness of the elderly.
Ha ha. I like you already, Miss Annie! I've never seen you around here before, have I?
I live in this house, but my masters never let me go out . . . until today.
I see . . . this is your first day of freedom . . . the big day!
Uh, yes. But why can't I go down to the street?
Minou and Chestnut went down to the street, and they were both seasoned warriors. They were both run over by cars.
OH!
I see . . . And you--you're so old . . . have you never gone down to the street?
Oh, sure, I've gone down, and I've come back again. But very carefully, because I have experience. I'll show you.
My house is over there. My master is an old philosopher who thinks lots of thoughts, but sometimes forgets to stop thinking and give me dinner.
Come on, follow me. You must meet Miss Rostropovna!
What are "cars"?

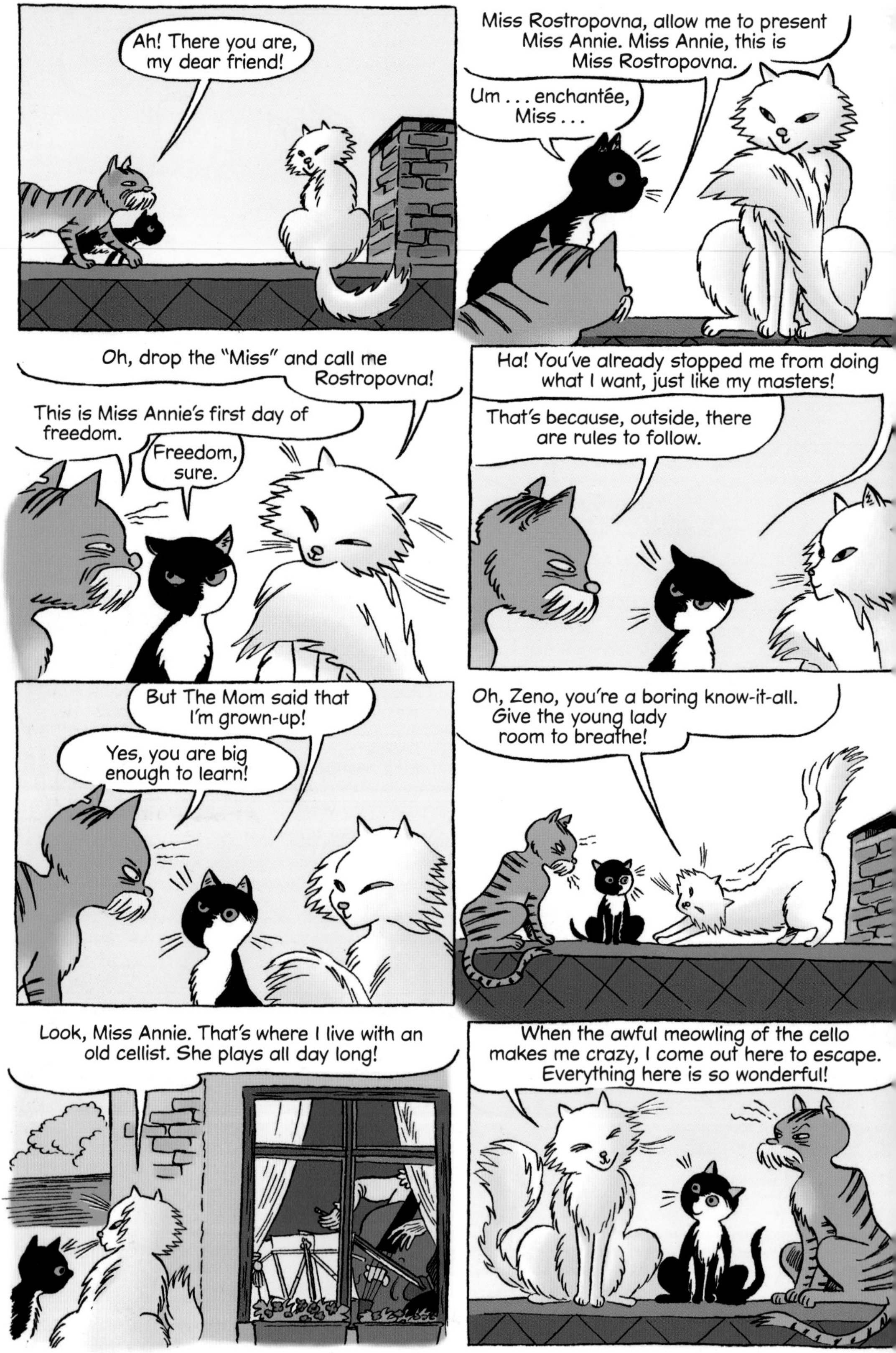
Ah! There you are, my dear friend!
Miss Rostropovna, allow me to present Miss Annie. Miss Annie, this is Miss Rostropovna.
Um . . . enchantée, Miss . . .
Oh, drop the "Miss" and call me Rostropovna!
This is Miss Annie's first day of freedom.
Freedom, sure.
Ha! You've already stopped me from doing what I want, just like my masters!
That's because, outside, there are rules to follow.
But The Mom said that I'm grown-up!
Yes, you are big enough to learn!
Oh, Zeno, you're a boring know-it-all. Give the young lady room to breathe!
Look, Miss Annie. That's where I live with an old cellist. She plays all day long!
When the awful meowling of the cello makes me crazy, I come out here to escape. Everything here is so wonderful!

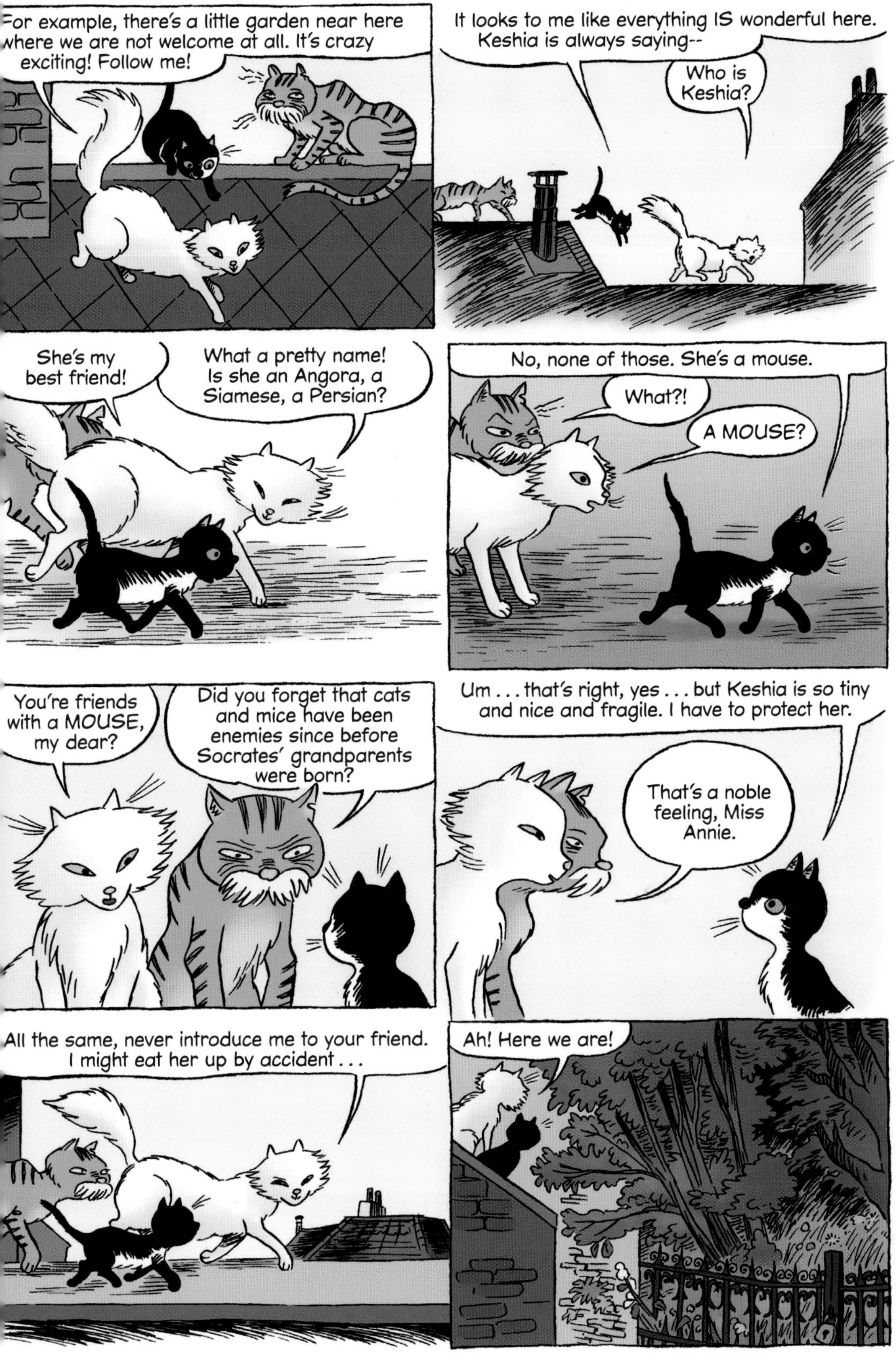
For example, there's a little garden near here where we are not welcome at all. It's crazy exciting! Follow me!
It looks to me like everything IS wonderful here. Keshia is always saying--
Who is Keshia?
She's my best friend!
What a pretty name! Is she an Angora, a Siamese, a Persian?
No, none of those. She's a mouse.
What?!
A MOUSE?
You're friends with a MOUSE, my dear?
Did you forget that cats and mice have been enemies since before Socrates' grandparents were born?
Um . . . that's right, yes . . . but Keshia is so tiny and nice and fragile. I have to protect her.
That's a noble feeling, Miss Annie.
All the same, never introduce me to your friend. I might eat her up by *accident* . . .
Ah! Here we are!

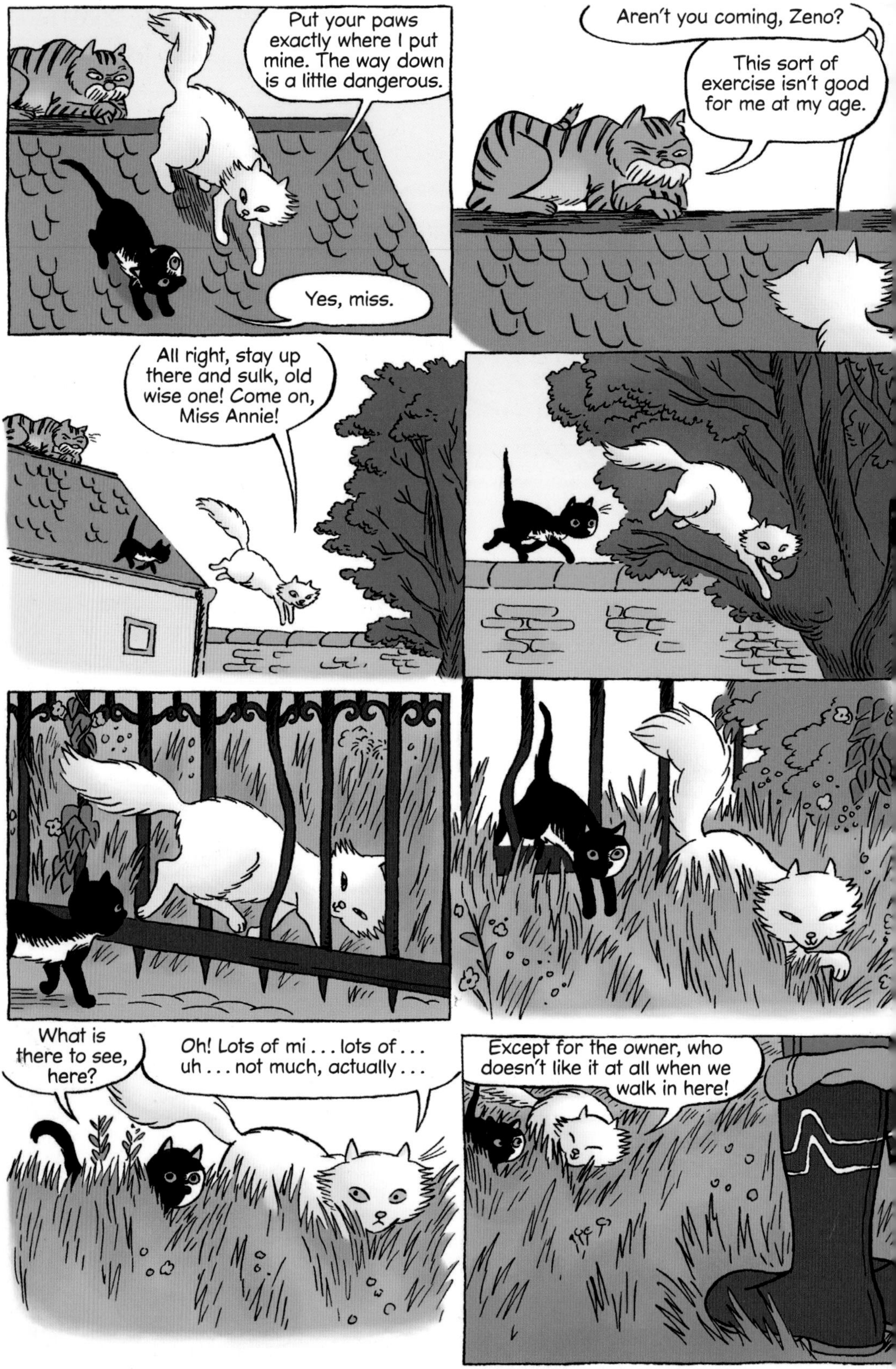

Put your paws exactly where I put mine. The way down is a little dangerous.
Yes, miss.
Aren't you coming, Zeno?
This sort of exercise isn't good for me at my age.
All right, stay up there and sulk, old wise one! Come on, Miss Annie!
What is there to see, here?
Oh! Lots of mi . . . lots of . . . uh . . . not much, actually . . .
Except for the owner, who doesn't like it at all when we walk in here!

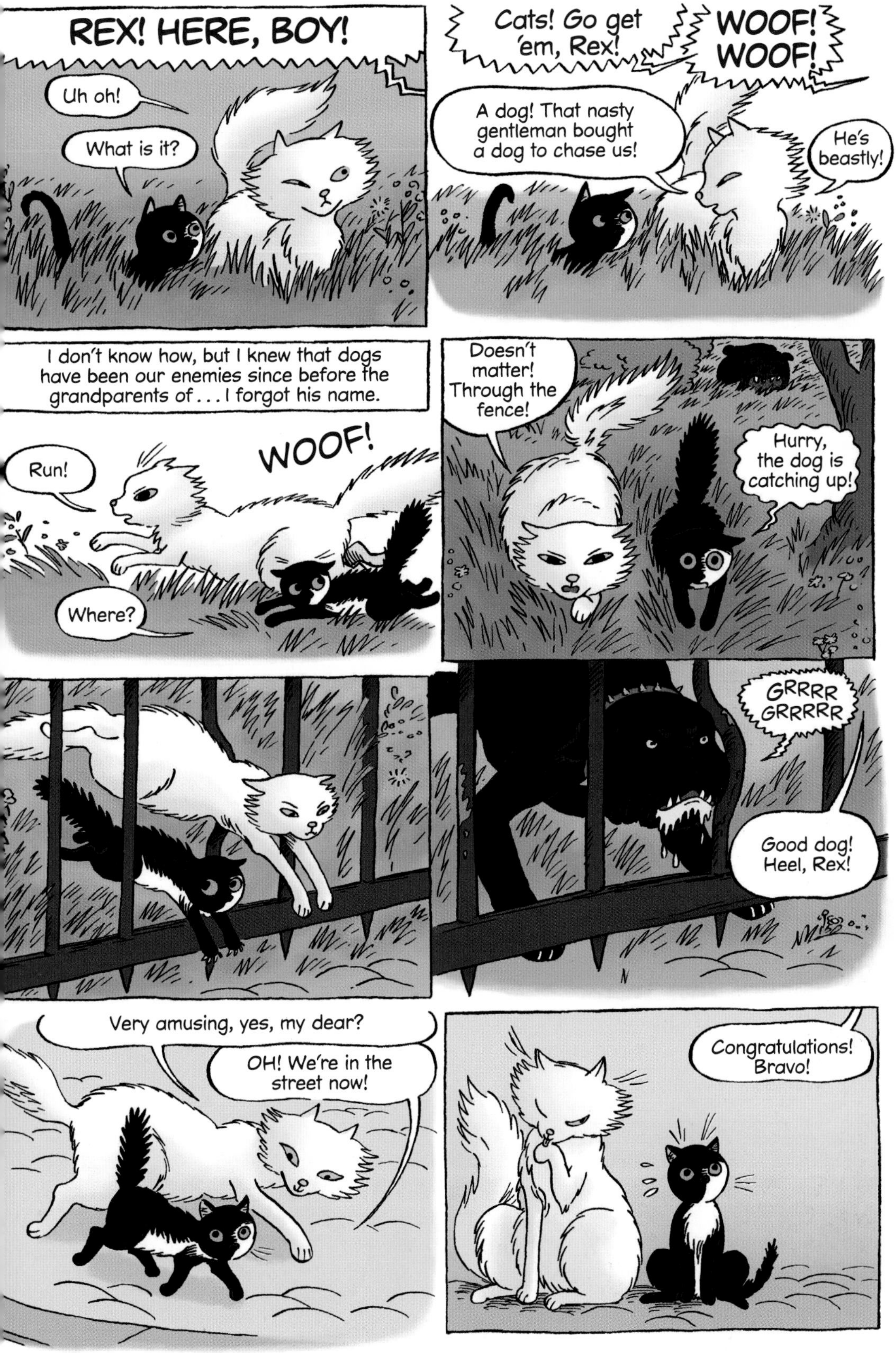
REX! HERE, BOY!
Uh oh!
What is it?
Cats! Go get 'em, Rex!
WOOF! WOOF!
A dog! That nasty gentleman bought a dog to chase us!
He's beastly!
I don't know how, but I knew that dogs have been our enemies since before the grandparents of . . . I forgot his name.
Run!
WOOF!
Where?
Doesn't matter! Through the fence!
Hurry, the dog is catching up!
GRRRR GRRRRR
Good dog! Heel, Rex!
Very amusing, yes, my dear?
OH! We're in the street now!
Congratulations! Bravo!

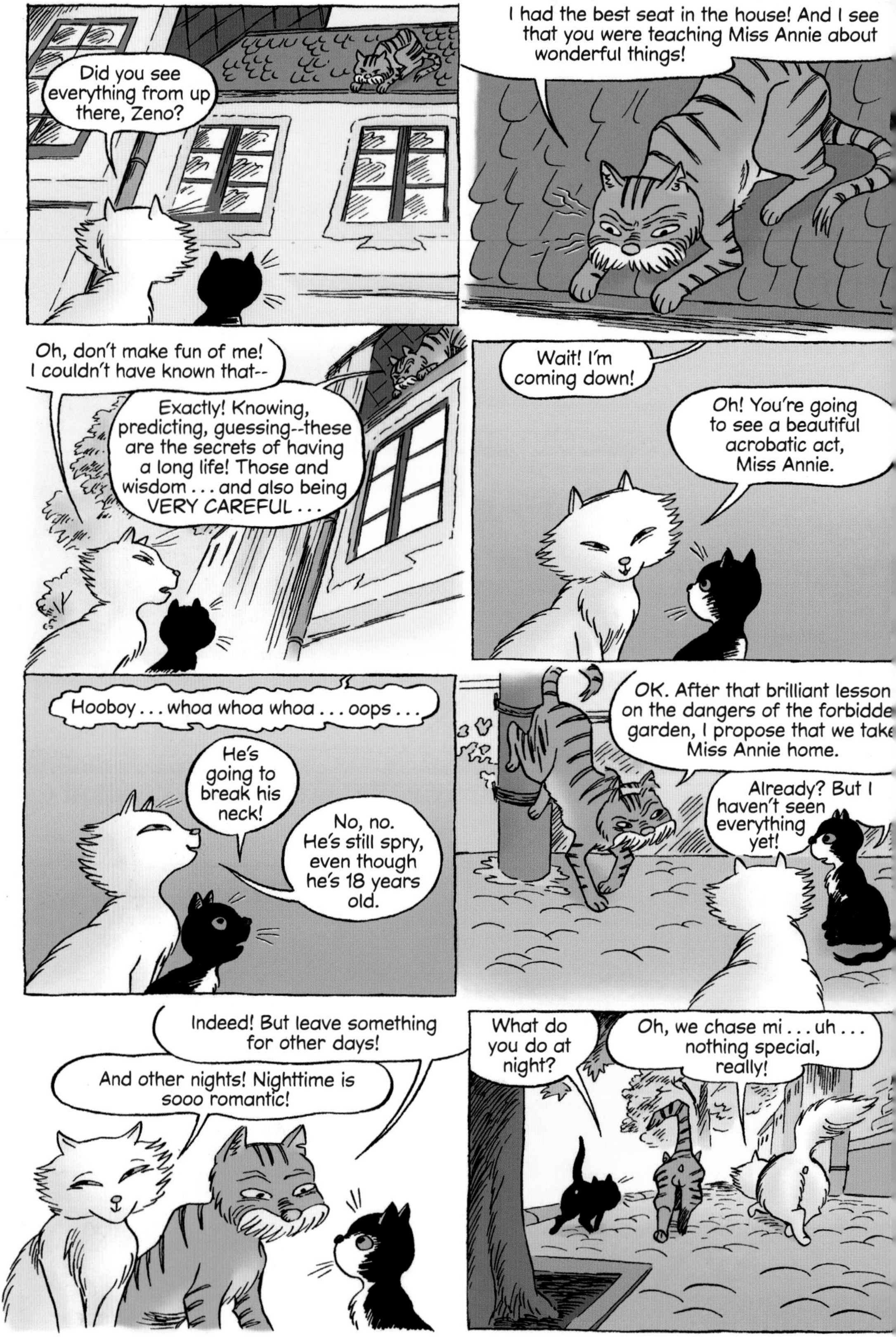
Did you see everything from up there, Zeno?
I had the best seat in the house! And I see that you were teaching Miss Annie about wonderful things!
Oh, don't make fun of me! I couldn't have known that--
Exactly! Knowing, predicting, guessing--these are the secrets of having a long life! Those and wisdom . . . and also being VERY CAREFUL . . .
Wait! I'm coming down!
Oh! You're going to see a beautiful acrobatic act, Miss Annie.
Hooboy . . . whoa whoa whoa . . . oops . . .
He's going to break his neck!
No, no. He's still spry, even though he's 18 years old.
Already? But I haven't seen everything yet!
Indeed! But leave something for other days!
And other nights! Nighttime is sooo romantic!
What do you do at night?
Oh, we chase mi . . . uh . . . nothing special, really!

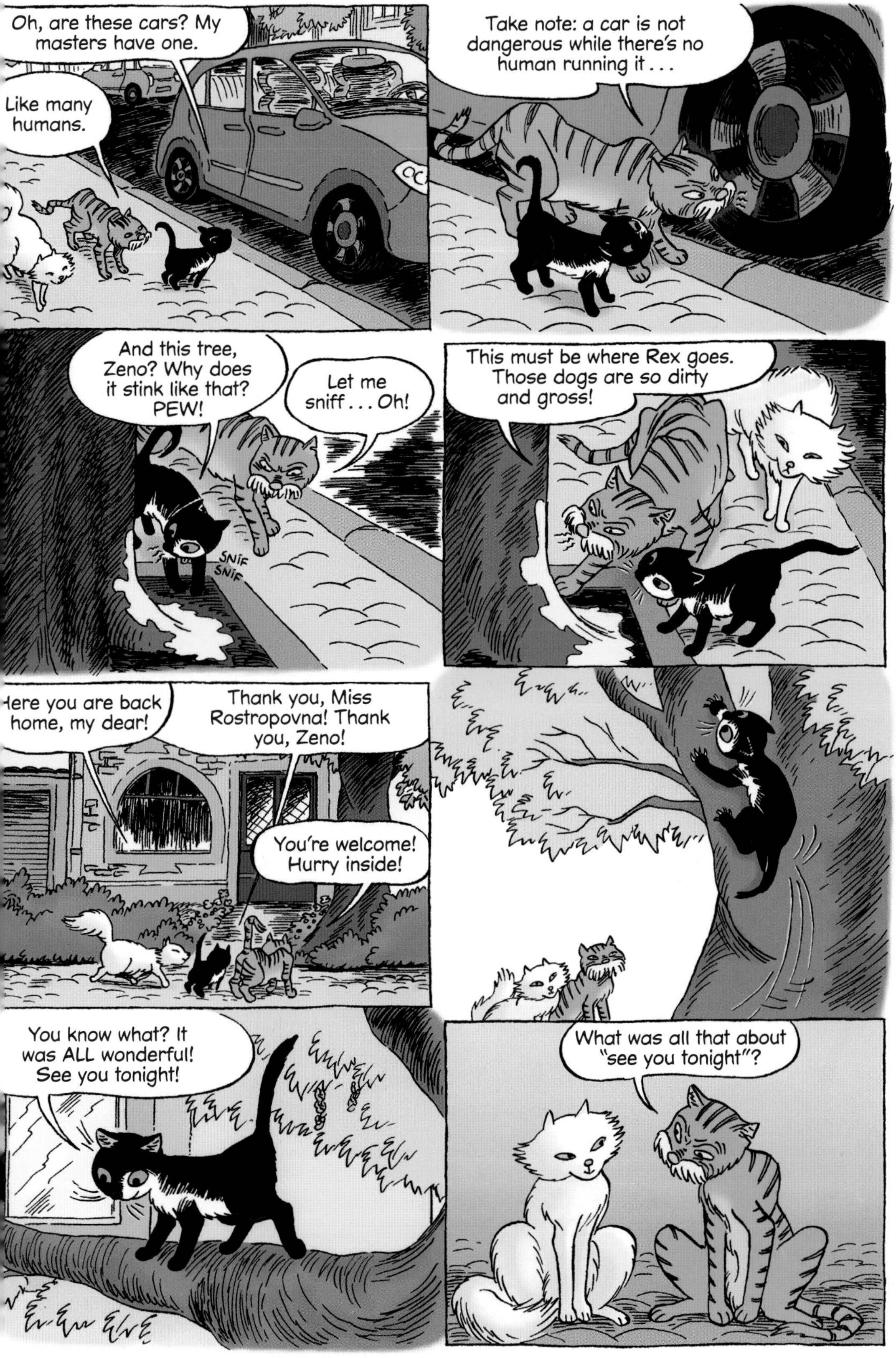
Oh, are these cars? My masters have one.
Like many humans.
Take note: a car is not dangerous while there's no human running it . . .
And this tree, Zeno? Why does it stink like that? PEW!
Let me sniff . . . Oh!
SNIF SNIF
This must be where Rex goes. Those dogs are so dirty and gross!
Here you are back home, my dear!
Thank you, Miss Rostropovna! Thank you, Zeno!
You're welcome! Hurry inside!
You know what? It was ALL wonderful! See you tonight!
What was all that about "see you tonight"?

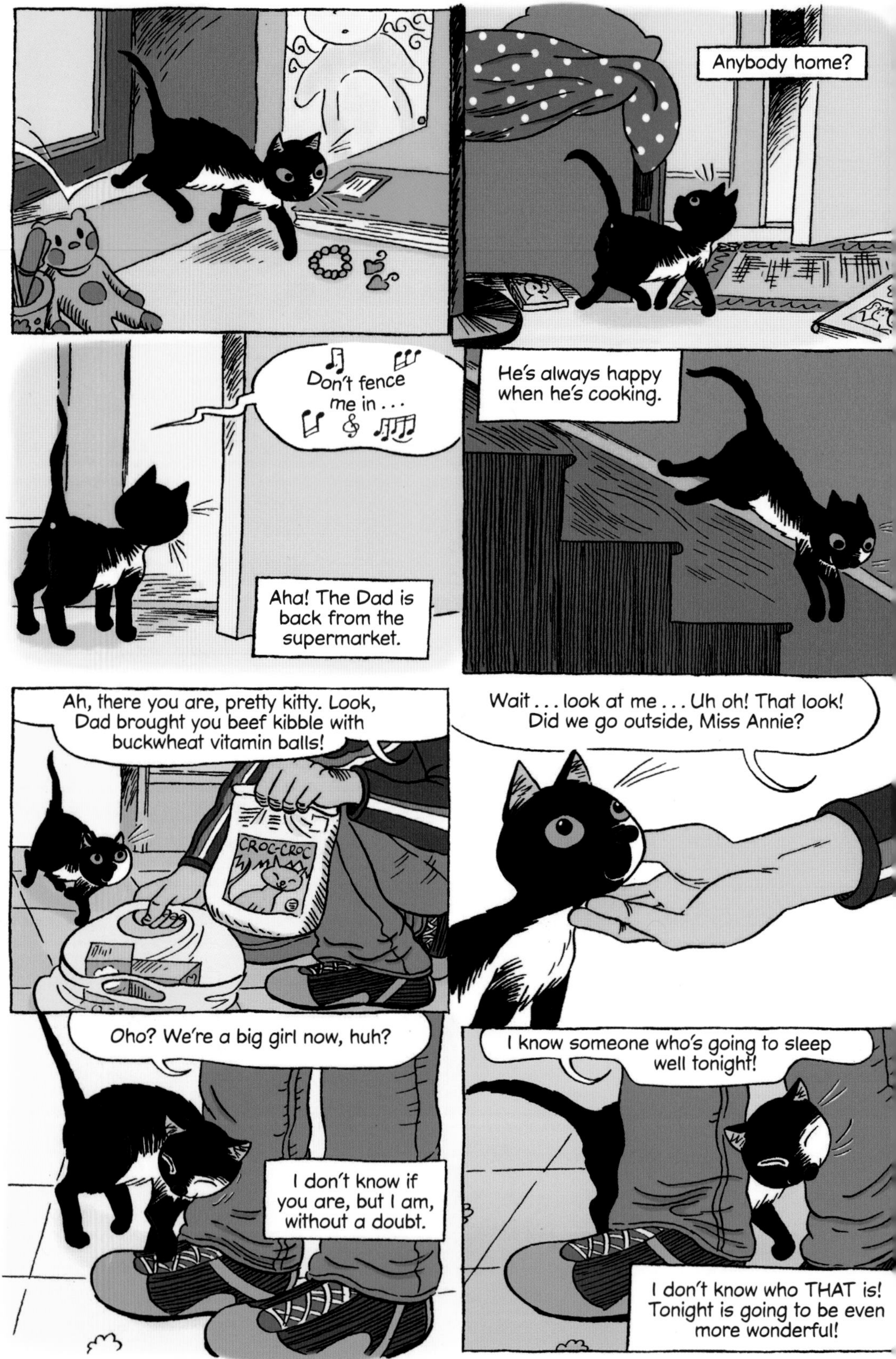
Anybody home?
Don't fence me in . . .
Aha! The Dad is back from the supermarket.
He's always happy when he's cooking.
Ah, there you are, pretty kitty. Look, Dad brought you beef kibble with buckwheat vitamin balls!
CROC-CROC
Wait . . . look at me . . . Uh oh! That look! Did we go outside, Miss Annie?
Oho? We're a big girl now, huh?
I don't know if you are, but I am, without a doubt.
I know someone who's going to sleep well tonight!
I don't know who THAT is! Tonight is going to be even more wonderful!

The End